THE BIRCHWOOD PARK MURDERS

THE BIRCHWOOD PARK MURDERS

By J.L. Anderson

The Birchwood Park Murders, Copyright © 2021 by J.L Anderson.

All rights reserved.

This is a work of fiction. Names, characters, places, and incidents either are the product of the author's imagination or are used fictitiously, and any resemblance to an actual person, living or dead, business companies, events, or locales is entirely coincidental.

No part of this book may be reproduced, stored in a retrieval system or transmitted in any form or by any means (electronic, mechanical, photocopying, recording or otherwise) without express written permission of the publisher.

First Printing: June 2021

ISBN: 978-1-946195-97-5

Library of Congress Number: 2021911286

Cover Photograph by Wade T. Anderson

Cover and Interior Design: FuzionPress

Published by FuzionPress

1250 East 115th Street, Burnsville, MN 55337

In loving memory of Barbara Davis Reiss

CHAPTER 1

He hopped off the asphalt trail and ran across the meadow. "Come on," he called.

She watched him move sure-footedly over the fresh grass, then threw up her arms and trotted off after him. "Where are you going?"

He stopped at the edge of the woods and gestured with a thumb over his shoulder. "In there."

She looked past him into the shadowy forest. "But, why?"

He grinned wide. "It will be fun."

She looked at him doubtfully, but her twitterpated teenage heart knew she'd follow him anywhere.

He pushed through the brush and entered the woods. "Through here."

"Okay," she said. "But I don't think this is a good idea."

Despite her objection, he continued on.

She watched as he maneuvered nimbly through the thicket. The afternoon sun filtered down through the leaves and danced on the forest floor. Sprouts popped up through the ground, their buds almost ready to bloom. A robin picked up a twig, flew up into the trees to its nest and secured it inside.

He ventured deeper, his long strides increasing the distance between them.

"Slow down," she said as she made her way through the tangled woods after him.

He stepped up on a boulder with his lanky legs and peered over the foliage. Grasping a nearby branch, he raised to his toes. "Over there." He pointed ahead.

She crouched low, slipping past an enormous swarm of gnats, and moved in next to the large rock. "I hate bugs," she said.

"Just a little bit farther."

The bright daylight streamed down through the opening in the canopy. She shielded her eyes with her hand and squinted up at him. "Promise?"

The sunbeams produced a halo around his head. "Promise." He hopped down. "This way," he said, continuing into the woods.

She pulled up her hood and pushed onward, the twigs that covered the ground crunched under her feet.

He ducked under a fallen tree trunk that had caught in the crotch of another, forming a low archway.

A huge crow, with feathers so black they looked blue, perched on a branch and cackled angrily at them.

He picked up a rock and threw it into the tree. "Get out of here you stupid crow!" He picked up another and took aim. The crow flew off. "He won't bother us now."

She smiled at her protector. She wasn't going to worry about what the other girls thought. *She* couldn't help it if he chose her over Jessica. She slipped under the archway after him.

"Over here," he said as he pushed past a long branch. It swung back and hit her in the face.

"Ow!" she cried.

He stopped and looked back to see what had happened. "Oh sorry. You've got to watch out for that."

She touched her cheek, then wiped the blood on her fingertips onto her jeans. "I'm bleeding."

"It's just a scratch. You'll be okay."

"This is not fun."

He smirked. "But it will be." He stopped in a clearing on the other side and held his arms wide. "This is a good spot."

She stepped out into the opening after him. "A good spot? For what?"

He grinned again.

She scrunched up her nose. "It stinks back here."

He moved closer to her and slid the hood off her hair.

She slapped at a black fly that landed on her neck. "What are you doing?"

"Making your dreams come true."

He reached his lips for hers, but she pushed him away.

"No," she said. "Wait."

"Wait?" He rolled his eyes. "For what?"

She leaned down and slapped at another black fly on her ankle. "Geez, what's with these flies?"

"Come on," he urged. "Just one kiss."

"No," she said again. "And what is that smell?"

"Come on," he encouraged. "I think you'll like it."

She held up her hands to ward him off. "Look, John. I'm, I'm sorry." She took a breath. The words caught in her throat, but she knew she had to say them. She looked sheepishly into his face. "I'm just not ready for that."

He stared silently at her for a long moment. Then he sighed. He picked up a stick and tossed it into the woods. "Hey, don't worry. It's okay."

"Thanks." She dropped her hands to her sides.

He took a step toward her. "Is this your first date?"

She nodded.

He moved closer. "Then I'm glad you're here with me."

She crinkled her brow. "Thank you."

He brushed the hair from her face, and looked at her tenderly. "Don't worry," he said again. "It will be fine."

Her heart raced. He was so close. It was frightening. Thrilling. Confusing. "But I –"

"Don't you like me?"

"Well sure, but –"

He took her by the waist and whispered into her ear. "Please? Just one?"

She felt dizzy. Delirious. Her resolve crumbled. "Okay, just one."

His lips locked on to hers and his hands began to creep up from her waist.

She pushed them down. "Stop it!" she protested. She tried to get away, but his grip was tight.

"Come on. Just a little feel."

"No!" She pried his fingers back. "Stop it!"

"Come on."

"No!" She struggled to get loose.

He smirked. "Jessica lets me."

The words pierced her adolescent heart like a knife. "What?" She pulled back and slapped his face hard, yanking herself free. "Then go back to Jessica!"

She turned to run, but before her second stride, she tripped over a rock that was jutting up from the forest floor, and she fell to the ground.

Her hand hit first, landing on the man's large shoe. She pulled her hand away quickly and sat back on her calves. Her eyes moved up the length of his long body to his face and she screamed.

CHAPTER 2

Isaac tucked his notepad into his jacket pocket, got out of the car and took a moment to feel the sun on his face. After off and on snow flurries throughout April, he thought spring would never arrive. But May was now here in all its glory. After a long, cold winter, the world was reborn. The naked winter branches were again clothed in green. The water flowed, reflecting the blue of the sky. Tulips, hyacinths and crocuses popped up from gardens releasing their heavenly fragrance into the air. For the rest of the United States, and according to the Gregorian calendar, the new year began in January, but for Isaac, a lifelong Minnesotan, the new year began in spring.

Isaac looked up and down the parkway and saw nothing but police cars. He rubbed his forehead. *Here we go again*, he thought to himself. They told him the body had been there a while. He groaned at the thought. The cases that involved old corpses were always the hardest. Sure, the coroner could usually figure out how the person died, and through dental records and missing person reports, the police could usually figure out who the person was. But who committed the crime and why? Those were the big questions.

Evidence also became much harder to find. And the more time that had passed, the more difficult it became. Important clues that may have been carelessly, accidently or unknowingly dropped by a perpetrator could have blown away or washed away over time.

Isaac stepped onto the sidewalk that ran parallel to the road around the parkway and saw Tom heading his direction. He waved. "Hey Tom!"

"Hey Jefe!" Tom responded.

"Heffay?" Isaac asked.

"Jefe," Tom repeated. "I started Spanish classes. It means boss."

"Spanish classes?" How Tom fit that in with all his other activities, Isaac had no idea. In the short month Isaac had known him, he didn't think he'd seen Tom sit down once. Tom became his new partner when his last partner, Vick, finally made good on his threat and moved to California.

"Yep. So when I go hang gliding in Peru I can communicate with the locals."

"Of course." Isaac had taken some Spanish in high school, but that was a long time ago. "Have you seen the body?"

Tom shook his head. "Not yet, but I've heard it's not pretty."

"Hopefully most of the dirty work has been taken care of."

As if on cue, they watched as a petite, sinuous woman emerged from the woods ahead of them. Isaac recognized her immediately. He grinned and put a hand on Tom's shoulder. "Tom, there's someone I'd like you to meet." He turned and headed toward her. "Cynthia!"

Tom followed.

She pulled some leaves from her silky, black hair. "Isaac, I'm so glad you're here. This one is going to need a good detective."

Isaac smiled. "Nice to see you too, Cynthia." *So far so good.*

She bent over and brushed some dirt off the knees of her pants. "I HATE HATE HATE working with those other idiots at your station." She straightened up and glared at Tom.

Tom reflexively took a step back.

Isaac chuckled. Cynthia always had that effect on people.

"And the officer cordoning off the scene is a big, fat buffoon." She leaned back and looked Isaac up and down. "Looks like you could drop a few pounds yourself, Isaac."

"Ouch," Tom said under his breath.

Isaac couldn't help but smile at Tom's reaction. It was the usual reaction people had when first meeting Cynthia. She was a dichotomy. She had the look of soft velvet, but the touch of extra-course sandpaper. "How nice of you to notice, Cynthia," Isaac responded. "Good advice. Thank you."

"Always happy to help a friend." She smiled at him. "Don't worry about it too much, that happens when you get old."

Tom's mouth dropped open.

"In your forties now?" she asked.

Isaac nodded. "You're spot on as always, Cynthia. I'll be forty-one in June."

"Just lay off the dessert for a while, then you'll be back in shape."

She turned toward Tom.

Tom took another step back.

"I tell him that because I like him," she explained.

Isaac smiled at Tom. "She likes me."

"That's a new twist on Minnesota Nice," Tom said.

"It depends on your definition of "nice," she said. "Is it nice to turn a blind eye to those who clearly need your assistance? Is it nice not to tell someone they have spinach in their teeth? Is it nice to let someone walk around with a tag hanging out of their shirt? Is it nice not to tell Lorraine over there that her application of blush makes her look like a clown?" She reached over and pat Isaac's stomach that was at about the same height as her head. "Isaac needed my assistance."

Tom smiled at that. "Are you always this direct?"

"Yes," she said matter-of-factly. "As a petite and beautiful woman, I find it's the only way to get people to listen to me."

Tom blinked, unable to find any words.

"Our bodies are our vehicles," she continued. "It's important to take care of them." She took a moment and slowly scrutinized Tom. "I can see you take care of yours."

"Um—" he stammered. "Thank you?" He looked at Isaac with pleading eyes.

"Tom," Isaac interjected, rescuing Tom from further discomfort. "This is Cynthia Chu, one of our finest Hennepin County Medical Examiners. Cynthia, this is Tom Bryant, my new partner. He's from Wisconsin."

Cynthia held out her hand to Tom. "*The* finest, really."

Tom cautiously took her tiny hand. "Good to know."

She clasped her left hand on top of his and held tight. "Just like Isaac here is the finest detective on the force."

Tom had to agree with that statement. He'd learned more in the last four weeks working with Isaac than in his last five years on the force.

She released his hand and stood back. "Whatever you're doing, Tom, keep it up. It's working." She winked at him. "I know bodies. It's what I do for a living."

She turned toward the woods with purpose. "Come with me." She stepped into the forest and began retracing her steps as Isaac and Tom trailed behind.

"What do we know?" Isaac asked.

She slipped between some small saplings. "It was definitely a homicide. Large hole in the stomach. Most likely a gunshot wound."

Isaac, twice Cynthia's height, pulled the tree branches back and held them so that he and Tom could follow. The foliage was that bright spring green that looked like it was right out of a children's drawing. Little purple flowers covered the forest floor.

"The body was covered with brush, so we had to pull that away," she told them, then effortlessly hurdled over a fallen tree trunk.

Tom vaulted over after her.

"That fat officer was quite clumsy about it. I hope it doesn't cause problems with your investigation."

Isaac sat on the tree trunk and it cracked under his weight. He pulled one leg over and then the other. With both feet on the ground, he pushed off and hustled along the trail to catch up to the others.

"I made sure they got lots of pictures."

Isaac pulled out a tissue and wiped his brow.

"The body has been here a while. Most likely two and a half to three months."

Isaac caught up and fell in behind them. "Two and a half to three months?"

"Yes. But the cold weather appears to have severely retarded the process of putrefaction." She stepped out into the clearing.

Tom followed right behind. He held back the brush to let Isaac through.

Cynthia walked over to the body frightening a crow attempting to get a little snack. It flew up and perched in a nearby tree. "The cold also inhibited any immediate insect activity. Looks like the maggots didn't move in for a few months." She pointed at the mid-section. "But they are certainly at home there now."

Isaac could see the movement of the wormlike insects and did his best not to gag.

The crow looked down hungrily.

She moved to the head of the body. "Some rodent damage, particularly to the face and hands. But we should be able to get a good cast of the teeth."

A black fly landed on Tom's arm causing an involuntarily shiver. He slapped it hard and it fell to the ground. He pulled down his sleeves and crossed his arms over his chest.

"As you can see, there's also been some carnivore activity to the right leg."

Isaac stepped toward the corpse's midsection.

The crow startled, then settled on a higher branch.

Isaac noted the missing femur and then visually measured the distance from the shoes to the head. "He looks tall."

Cynthia nodded. "I would estimate your height or even taller, Isaac. Maybe six foot, three inches or so."

The crow cackled angrily causing them all to look up. A competitor had landed on a nearby branch. The new arrival puffed up, rapidly flapped its outstretched wings and held its ground.

Tom took advantage of the interruption and kept his eyes toward the birds.

"Caucasian?" Isaac asked.

"Well, there's not much skin left on the face and the skin on his arms and legs has adhered to the clothing, but yes, I believe he's Caucasian," Cynthia answered.

"You said you thought he'd been here a few months?"

"Well yes, you can see fluids being purged and a large number of worms and moist putrefied tissue mass in the thoracic cavity."

Tom turned a little pale, stepped back, and covered his mouth with his hands.

"And some putty-like putrefied flesh is pouring out from the abdomen."

"T-M-I, Cynthia," Tom said. "T-M-I."

Until this moment, Isaac had successfully looked at the scene analytically. He turned away and did his best to stifle his churning stomach.

"I'm just answering Isaac's question," Cynthia responded to Tom, indifferent to their discomfort. "That would indicate Stage IV," she continued. "Putting the estimated date of death at around . . ."

Isaac took a cleansing breath and turned back around. "February 15," he said.

Cynthia's mouth snapped shut. Tom's hands dropped from his face. They both stared at Isaac.

Isaac pulled out a tissue and wiped his mouth. "Well," he clarified, "February 15 or very shortly thereafter."

"What?" Cynthia asked. "I don't even have him on the table yet."

"From the height and size of the body I can be 80 percent sure," he explained. "But, because I remember those." Isaac pointed at the shoes. "I can be 99 percent sure." He looked back and forth between them. "It's Garrett Holt."

CHAPTER 3

Isaac and Tom managed their way back out of the woods by aiming for the sound of the traffic on the Parkway.

Tom stepped carefully through some prickly brush along the edge and out into the open. "Man, how did they ever get to that spot?" he asked rhetorically, referring to the hikers who found the body.

Isaac ducked under a low branch and came out behind him. He rubbed his hands over his head to clear any leaves. "Where are they now?"

Tom pulled a twig off of his jacket. "In a squad car in the parking lot."

Without the canopy of the trees, it felt much warmer. Isaac unzipped his jacket. "Alright, let's go see them," he said as they descended the hill to the sidewalk.

Tom looked uneasily back over his shoulder, making sure Cynthia wasn't within earshot. "Well, that was disturbing."

Isaac pulled out his sunglasses. "Which part?"

"Which part? Are you kidding me? Let's just say it's a blanket statement." He held up his pointer finger. "For starters, I've never seen a body in that condition before." A shiver ran up his spine. "I'll have nightmares for a week."

Isaac nodded. "Yeah, me too." But he'd been doing this long enough to know that sleepless nights were just part of the job. This crime scene was particularly gruesome, but other crime scenes had been equally earth-shattering and probably more tragic, like the little two-year old who had been shaken to death by a care-giver. Years later, that memory still caused him sleepless nights. In this line of work, in the end, no matter the situation, it was always just bad. The good only came when justice was done. But Isaac had to admit to himself, it was still never enough.

Tom grimaced. "Did you see those maggots?"

"Don't remind me. I was going to make Claudia my favorite orzo pasta, but not now, not tonight." Isaac had taken over some of the cooking duties since his wife, Claudia, had recently returned to practicing law.

The thought of food made Tom's stomach churn. He'd forgo dinner tonight. Only an intense workout could shake the heebie-geebies of today. "And Cynthia was relentless," he continued. "Seeing the body was bad enough. I didn't need a detailed description of the decay. I thought I was going to lose it right there."

"She is very. . ." Isaac looked up to the clear blue sky and searched for the right word. "Thorough."

Tom groaned. "I guess that's one way to put it."

Isaac shrugged. "What can I say, she is very good at her job."

"She sure thinks highly of you," Tom said. "Although if the words hadn't come directly out of her own mouth, I would have never guessed it after she told you you were fat and old."

Isaac grinned at Tom. "She likes me." He slapped Tom's shoulder. "I think she likes you too."

"She scares me."

"She's available."

"Not surprised."

"You should ask her out."

"I'd rather stick my head in a meat grinder."

Isaac laughed. "But you two have so much in common."

Tom leered at him. "I think I take offense to that, Jefe."

"You're both so fit. You can take her rock climbing. Heck, you could probably carry her on your back. She only weighs about fifty pounds. Or how about skydiving? You wouldn't even know she was there."

"Oh, I'd know she was there, because she wouldn't shut up. She's like a wasp. You try to shoo her away but she keeps droning on until she finally lands the sting."

"She just has an inferiority complex."

"How in the world do you figure that? If anything, she has a superiority complex."

"She's intelligent and beautiful."

"She's insensitive and blunt." Tom crossed his arms over his chest. "And you know, Jefe, that's just enough of that. I told you, I have no desire to date anyone right now. And I can assure you, that I will *never* have a desire to date Cynthia. So, can we please stop?"

"Fine." Isaac had only been teasing about Cynthia after all, but why a young, smart, active man like Tom wasn't looking for a mate to share his time with, was a mystery to Isaac. He couldn't imagine life without Claudia. She was the reason he got up every morning. His reason for everything, really. Claudia and their three children, that is. What a blessing they were. "But you're gonna need somebody sometime, Tom."

Tom shook his head. "Give it up, Jefe. So," he said, changing the subject. "Who is this Garrett Holt?"

Isaac let out a long sigh. "Garrett Holt was the estranged husband of Crystal Holt who was found dead last Valentine's Day. Mr. Holt went missing just after we interviewed him about the murder."

Tom raised his eyebrows. "Just after you interviewed him?"

"Yeah, we had a tail on him, but lost him."

He raised his eyebrows higher. "Lost him?"

"Yeah." Isaac rubbed the back of his neck. "Don't go there. It's a sore spot."

Tom held up his hands as if he were under arrest. "Okay."

"Anyway, he was a suspect for a while, but an acquaintance actually committed the crime. According to the acquaintance, Mr. Holt gambled and was deep in debt. We should start sniffing around the bookies for more information."

"Got it."

The police were never able to determine exactly how Garrett left the coffee shop that day, shaking the tail, but Isaac had always suspected he didn't leave of his own free will. And the way they found him certainly confirmed his assumption. He looked over at his partner. "So, tell me about the hikers who found the body."

"I wouldn't call them hikers, really. Just a couple of kids out in the woods."

"Kids?" Isaac grimaced. "How old?"

"Teenagers," he assured him. "Well, okay, *young* teenagers."

"What were they doing back there?"

Tom laughed. "Seriously, Jefe? You have to ask? They were making out. I mean, what else would a teenage boy and girl be doing back in the woods?"

"A boy and girl? You hadn't mentioned that." He may be in his forties, but he still remembered.

"Yeah." Tom moved his hands in a serpentine gesture. "Learning the moves."

Isaac rolled his eyes. "Is that what they told you?"

"No, but they were quite evasive on the subject. The boy kept glancing over at the girl as if he was worried she was going to spill, but she remained tight-lipped."

"Sounds right, then."

Isaac and Tom entered the parking lot which had been cordoned off from the public.

"So, what *is* their story?" Isaac asked.

"Just what you'd expect. They were hiking through the woods and the girl tripped over a rock and discovered the body."

"The girl discovered the body?"

"Actually . . ." Tom cringed. "She *landed* on the body."

Isaac winced. *Poor kid!* Seeing that grisly scene was hard enough for a seasoned veteran. That girl would definitely need help to get through this. Both of those kids would.

"Officers said her scream could be heard for miles."

Isaac sighed. "I'd like to talk with them. Where are they?"

"Over there. The squad car at the back."

Isaac looked back over his shoulder at the news crews parked end to end along the road behind the police tape, impatiently waiting for an update. A dead body in

Birchwood Park was big news and every single station wanted the scoop.

An officer stood guard next to the car as they approached. "Hey Isaac," he called.

"Hey Bill," Isaac responded. Isaac knew that the officers were doing the best they could to protect the kids from the reporters, but the kids had to feel unsettled stowed away in that small, jail-like space with the hard, plastic seats and the steel bars separating them from the front seat. "We'd like to talk with the witnesses."

"Sure thing," Bill said. "They're getting pretty antsy. They've been stuck here for almost an hour now."

Isaac tried to get a look at them, but the sun glinted against the car windows and made it impossible to see inside. "Can't we let them get some fresh air?"

"Gotta protect their privacy. They're minors. Every time I open the door, the cameras start rolling."

"Okay, would you please go shoo those camera crews away for us, Bill?"

"We've been trying, Isaac, but they just won't budge. First Amendment rights and all."

"Of course." Isaac scratched the back of his head. "Go tell them there will be a press conference down the road by the park entrance."

"There's going to be a press conference?"

"Maybe." Isaac shrugged. "Just distract them for a while. I'm going to let these kids out for a few minutes."

Bill nodded, picked up his megaphone and hustled toward the edge of the cordoned area.

Isaac and Tom watched as the reporters packed up the vans and started moving expeditiously the other direction.

Tom reached for the door handle. "If we can't get in touch with the parents soon, the counselors will bring them home and sit with them until the parents arrive."

"Good."

Tom pulled the door open and leaned inside. "Hey kids, this nice detective would like to talk with you."

A tall, lanky kid came out first. He looked about thirteen or fourteen years old. He had gel in his hair, peach fuzz on his lip, Air Jordan's on his feet and a chip on his shoulder.

"Hey son," Isaac said. "What's your name?"

"John Rogers."

He looked stressed. "Do you play basketball?" Isaac asked, trying to calm him.

"Yeah." John shoved his hands in the pockets of his J. Crew jacket. "When can we go home?"

"Just a few minutes, okay? Then I'll have an officer take you home."

"I — I didn't do anything wrong," he stuttered. "We were just, you know, ah, exploring back there. Why are you keeping us?"

"We just want to keep you safe."

"This sucks," John mumbled under his breath.

Isaac couldn't disagree. An adult would struggle with finding a dead body and then being locked up in a police car like a criminal for almost an hour. It had to be absolutely frightening for a kid. "Just a few more minutes," he promised.

Tom offered a hand to the young girl in the car. "Be careful past that door jam," he said.

Isaac watched her emerge. Sweet. Innocent. Cherub-faced. His jaw dropped open and his heart leapt into his throat. "Avery?"

"Hi Daddy."

CHAPTER 4

"Oh, Avery," Isaac moaned as he took her in his arms, the reality of it all hitting him like a locomotive. She was so tiny and fragile. So young and innocent. He felt the sting of tears begin to fill his eyes. Never in all his time on the force had a relative been a witness to a homicide he was investigating. Never had a relative ever known one of the victims. Never had a relative even known one of the suspects. Never, never, never had he expected his own daughter to step out of that car.

"He's your dad?" John Rogers exclaimed and put his hands to his head.

Avery buried her face in her father's large chest and burst into tears.

Isaac stroked her hair, struggling to quell his own tears.

"Your dad is a cop?" young Rogers asked with alarm.

Isaac didn't hear him. All he could hear was his daughter's distress. *Why did it have to be Avery that found the body? That fell on the body?* He cringed at the thought. It was more than he could stomach. "It's okay honey, Daddy's here."

"A cop?" John Rogers repeated. Had he known *that*, he never would have asked her out. He never would have even considered it. And, he'd make darn sure that all his buddies also knew this very important piece of information. He looked over at Avery. She'd never get another date.

"I want to go home," she sputtered.

"Of course, baby. I'll get you home." And the boy needed to go home too. Isaac looked to Tom who stood with his mouth agape, then over at the boy. "Tom, stop catching flies and take the young man home," Isaac instructed. "Wait with him there until his mother arrives."

"Sure, Jefe," Tom responded, startled by the turn of events and immediately regretting his earlier insinuations about what the kids had been doing in the woods. "Will do."

"No, no! Not to my mom's," John said to Tom. "She'll flip out. Take me to my dad's."

Tom nodded at him, noticing the light pink welt on the boy's left cheek. "Okay, son." He reached for the keys in his pocket, then looked up and saw Cynthia striding determinedly their way.

"Detective Bryant!" Cynthia called.

Tom pretended not to hear and moved quickly toward the boy. "Com'mon son. Let's get you home."

Cynthia ran up from behind him and put her tiny hand on his arm. "Detective Bryant, you can come with me to assist with my examination of the body." She made it sound as if he had just won the Publisher's Clearing House Sweepstakes.

The sound this idea evoked in Tom came out reflexively, "Eeuww." He looked to Isaac with wide eyes and noticed the almost imperceptible shake of Isaac's head. Message received. *Don't get on Cynthia Chu's bad side.* Tom took his cue and made an effort to cover up his initial reaction. "Eeuw-you are very kind to offer, Cynthia. But I need to get this young man home to his parents."

"My dad's," John Rogers reiterated emphatically. "Not my mom's."

Cynthia creased her brow and placed her hands defiantly on her hips. "Can't someone else do that?" She looked dismissively at the boy. "This is much more important."

Tom raised his eyebrows. Although he had only known Cynthia for no more than an hour, he wasn't surprised that Cynthia's genetic makeup totally lacked a mothering instinct or anything resembling compassion for another. "No, Cynthia, thank you." Tom said firmly. "Not this time." *Not ever*, is what he wanted to say.

She placed her hand on his arm again, this time gripping tightly. "I don't think you understand. I'm offering you a front row seat."

This woman was something else. "Listen, Cynthia," Tom began.

Isaac's ears perked up. He hadn't heard that tone from Tom before. "He needs to get the kid home, Cynthia."

Tom wrangled his arm free from Cynthia's clench and set it on the boy's shoulder.

"My orders." Isaac brushed Avery's hair from her face and gently led her toward his car.

Cynthia watched Isaac and Avery walk away. "He shouldn't be holding the girl like that."

"It's his daughter," Tom explained.

"Oh," she said, then she turned her head and narrowed her eyes evilly at the boy.

John Rogers took a step back.

A shiver ran down Tom's spine. "Gotta go," he said escorting the boy away from the scene.

Cynthia called after him. "Your loss!"

CHAPTER 5

Nikki heard a whistle as she stepped out the door of Boulevard Wine and Spirits with bags in hand. "Hey, mama," said a young punk with a pock marked face and too much bravado.

"Get lost little boy," she said.

She cradled the bottle of wine in her right arm, resting the bag of goat cheese and crackers on top, and ambled down the sidewalk toward the bike rack.

The sun was beginning it's decent to the west, but there were still several hours of light left in the day to fit in an evening run. This was turning out to be a great weekend. Tucker had gone on a fundraising trip to Madden's Resort in Nisswa to rub shoulders with all his daddy's rich friends, and she was free to do whatever she pleased. No one would be around to tell her that her behavior was "unacceptable" or to just keep her mouth shut. Nikki was not and would never ever be a "Stepford Wife" and all their priggish carping and condescension made her even more determined to hang on to her individuality whenever possible. Without them around, she was free to let her hair down, or, in this case, spike it up.

Who did they think they were, anyway? She found it so hypocritical how that hoity-toity crowd looked down upon the townspeople who lived and worked in Greater Minnesota considering them nothing more than provincial hicks, but when those same arrogant assholes wanted to kick back and really enjoy themselves, Greater Minnesota is where they went. It was an idiosyncrasy that was well understood, universally derided, and totally exploited by those same "provincial hicks." They knew all too well who was wiser and were quite content to keep the stereotype going just enough to keep the money coming in. As Nikki's father was known to say with a big grin, "Those idiot "citi-ots" don't have a clue." It was the one thing they could agree on.

She stopped at the crosswalk at the end of the block.

"Need someone to share that with?" asked a voice from behind her.

She turned to find a fit thirty-something urban biker in tight fitting spandex straddling his red Salsa Warroad. *A decent bike for city travel*, she supposed. She ran a hand through her short-cropped, flaxen hair, adjusted the spikes on her head, and gave him the once-over.

He flashed a seductive smile.

She pulled a bang slowly across her forehead. "Tempting, but no."

"No?"

She held up the ring finger of her left hand in a gesture that could have easily been mistaken for another, and showed the three carats that had been there for more than four years now. "Married."

He leaned back. "Whoa," he said. "I didn't mean any offense. Quite the opposite, really."

He was cute. "None taken."

"Hey, it never hurts to check, right?"

"No, it never hurts to check." And another time, *after* the election, she might have had a different answer.

The light turned green.

He focused in on her voluminous lips. "Lucky man," he said with a wink, then pushed off, crossed to the other side and continued down the sidewalk.

No, it most certainly hadn't been luck. It had taken careful planning, perseverance, and some Oscar Award winning acting for State Senator Rennicke and his family to accept a provincial hick with no college degree from the nether lands of Plummer's Point, Minnesota, into their fold.

In the end, the years of studying their behaviors paid off. Every spring Bowers Marine delivered the Rennicke's boat from storage and put their dock in, and Nikki helped the Rennicke's local cleaning ladies ready their cabin for the summer. Then the Rennicke's would arrive and spread their wealth around, and Nikki decided then and there that she wanted more than just a piece of it. She wanted it to be hers. So, she watched them. She scrutinized them. She noted how they dressed, what they ate, how they spoke, their mannerisms, and their slang. And then she practiced.

It hadn't taken much to get Tucker's attention in the beginning. Nikki had an unusual, exotic look, most likely attributable to the little bit of Eskimo sprinkled into her Swedish bloodline. She drew constant attention from men. But, she knew it would take much more than just her good looks for Tucker to fall hard enough for him to be willing to stand up to the powerful force that was his father.

In the end, the winning argument was that by being one of them, she could bring in the votes from Greater Minnesota, and votes brought power. Nikki had come to recognize that Senator Rennicke would more than likely sell his soul to the devil if it brought in votes. For Nikki, the union brought something much more tangible. Money. And lots of it.

As she approached the bike rack outside the salon, a gray-haired gentleman brushed past her loosening her grip on the paper bag.

"Hey," she snapped.

"So sorry, young lady. My apologies."

She snarled and readjusted the package securing it in the crook of her arm. "Just watch where you're going."

He cocked his head and a look of recognition came to his eyes. "Say," he said. "Don't I know you?"

She rolled her eyes. *They were all alike, no matter the age.* "In your dreams, old man." She let the backpack slide down her arm and set it next to her bike.

"I beg your pardon?"

"Beg all you want. It won't get you anywhere."

He swallowed back the insult. "No, really. I know you. Aren't you Tucker's wife?"

Uh oh. She bent over quickly, focusing in on the bike lock combination. "Who?"

"Tucker Rennicke. Aren't you his wife?" he asked. "I'm George Carlson. We met at the Jeremiah Program fundraiser." George remembered her distinctly because of all the rumors that had been swirling around about her, and more particularly because those rumors were not complementary.

She kept her head down and pulled the sunglasses from the front pocket of the back pack. "The what? I have no idea what you're talking about." She slid them on, covering her eyes. "Now move on, Grandpa."

But George didn't budge. "Funny. You look just like her."

She spun the diamond around her finger to her palm and clenched her fist around it. She had to get rid of him. "Getting a little senile, are we?"

He hadn't considered the rumors about her anything more than petty political posturing at the fundraiser, but it appeared he had been wrong. She was wretched. "You could be her twin," George said.

Why didn't he just go? "Stop harassing me and get back to the old folks home, you old dolt."

"Her evil twin," he added.

Pretentious geezer. She turned and gave him the finger.

George responded in kind and then continued down the sidewalk.

Damn. She had to watch out for that. Thankfully, she figured his age would make most pat him on the shoulder and put his story down to mistaken identity, but she had better be prepared to do some damage control. Fortunately, the Rennickes would never allow a divorce to taint their legacy. If she could keep Tucker happy, he could keep them mostly at bay.

She tucked the wine bottle into one side of the backpack and the cheese and crackers in the outer compartment, being careful not to damage her new nail extensions. She threw her backpack on and pulled her bright yellow Diamondback Haanjo out of the rack. *Now this was a bike made for rugged exploration.*

She took off, the wind rippling over her toned muscles. Riding in the city was quite different than riding in Plummer's Point. Minneapolis had a plethora of sidewalks, bike lanes and paved biking paths running in and around the city. Although touted as one of the five best in the nation for bikers, Nikki felt it stifling, controlling, and downright boring. *What was wrong with everyone?* They all followed the paths, no one strayed. People went where they were told they could go. Sure, Birchwood Park had some decent off-road cycling trails, but they were still government-sanctioned trails. Nothing along those paths hadn't already been discovered. There were no new wonders to find.

As much as she had wanted this life, she missed the unpaved countryside where you were not directed in any particular direction and were free to roam. No one told you where you could ride. There were no rules on the gravel roads and woodland trails. Of course, there were no guarantees that you wouldn't run into places that were difficult to traverse, and without roadmaps to follow, you had to take your chances. But that's the way life should be. Just do the best with what you have and improvise if necessary.

It was a short trip home around Lake of the Isles, to Cedar Lake Parkway, to their lovely turn of the century two-story Tudor, a home befitting the next Rennicke to hold public office. And thanks to Tucker's daddy's money, that's where they lived.

As she drew near, she saw a familiar face waiting on the stoop outside her door. Her heart skipped a beat.

CHAPTER 6

Isaac turned on the engine and let the cool air blow over them. His mind was reeling from the completely unexpected turn of events of the day. What had started out as a bad situation had most certainly become much worse.

Disquieting questions pitched about in his brain, bouncing back and forth between worry over Avery's physical health and her mental health, but both with one central focus: the loss of her innocence. For starters, who was that boy and what were they doing back in the woods? Had they been there before? And even more disturbing than his concerns about the boy, what effect would encountering that gruesome corpse have on such a young adolescent when he himself, a veteran homicide detective, could barely stomach the sight?

How was he to comfort her? What would Claudia do? Could the two of them soothe her fears? Could they handle the anxiety that was sure to surface? And just how would that anxiety manifest itself? What impact could this have on her life? He rubbed his hand over his head. He had no idea where to begin. He looked over at his first born. Surely she needed to release all the anguish that must be building up inside. He just needed to open the door.

Isaac leaned over and gently set his hand on hers. "Go ahead, Avery, let it out."

She turned away from him and stared out the side window. "I don't want to talk about it," she said resolutely.

He sat back in his seat. It was not what he had expected. For some reason, he thought the story would come spilling out like a waterfall out of control, and he had planned to be the dam to stop it, contain it, calm it, and give it some peace. But yet, she sat statue-like as if frozen in place.

Isaac reluctantly drew his hand back and put the car in drive. "Okay, honey." Perhaps she just needed time to herself to organize her thoughts and feelings. Respecting her wishes, they sat in silence the entire trip home.

Isaac pulled into the garage and closed the overhead door. "We're home now, sweetheart," he said. Even though he had stated the obvious, he hoped it would be reassuring to her. He walked around the car, opened the door and helped her out.

She walked as if in a daze.

Walter, their one-year-old, sixty-pound, mixed breed, knucklehead of a dog came leaping at them as they stepped into the house. Avery dropped to the cold, tile floor and pulled him close. Walter quieted immediately and leaned into her. It was remarkable how he seemed to sense her distress.

Isaac waited, ready to be there to help Avery get to wherever she wanted to go, but Walter settled into her lap and it appeared Avery was staying put. "I'm going to go give mom a call," he told her.

"Okay," she said.

He gave her a peck on the head and went to the kitchen to call Claudia.

Claudia picked up the phone on the first ring. "It must be pretty dull at the station for you to call me in the middle of the day," she said.

"No." He sighed. "I wouldn't say that."

She sat up straighter in her chair. "Isaac, what's wrong?" She knew instantly by the tone of his voice there was a problem. Even under the most stressful of circumstances, her stoic husband kept his cool.

How was he to tell her? He'd try, but there was really no way to ease into it. "Remember Garrett Holt?"

A shiver ran up her spine. How could she forget? Garrett Holt, the only visitor to the law firm they'd ever had to have forcibly removed. The husband of Crystal Holt, a very wealthy client, and heir to Crystal's fortune who took Crystal's attorney by the throat when she told him he didn't have full control over the inheritance his wife left him. "You're scaring me, Isaac. Is he back making threats? Do I need to alert building security?"

"No, no threats. I think we found his body."

A wave of relief came over her. "Man, you had me going there."

How he hated the words that were about to come out of his mouth. "Actually, Avery found the body."

She blinked. "What?" She felt suddenly sick. "What are you saying to me?"

"Avery and a friend were walking through Birchwood Park and they found a dead body. I'm pretty sure it's Garrett Holt." Not the whole truth, but he'd have time for that later. He could almost hear her heart beating through the phone line. This was more than enough information for now. Later he'd share the rest of the details, including who that "friend" was, where they were, and how she happened upon the body.

"Wait. Just wait." She was having trouble wrapping her head around this. Her baby had found a dead body? "This is too much."

Yes, it certainly is, Isaac thought to himself. "Can you come home?"

"On my way."

Isaac went back to the rear entry and found Avery still on the floor holding Walter. There was something so sweet about it, he almost wanted to take a picture. He squatted down next to them and patted Walter on his head. Avery just stared into the distance.

"Come on, honey," he said to her. "Let's get you off the floor." He lifted her up and carried her like he used to when she was a baby. *Where had those thirteen years gone?* He set her on the couch in the family room and sat on the coffee table across from her. Even though they all knew he wasn't allowed, Walter jumped up next to her and laid his head on Avery's lap. Avery pulled him closer. Sometimes rules can be broken, and this was one of those times.

"Mom's on her way home," Isaac told her.

"Okay," she said

"Is there anything I can get for you?"

Avery shook her head, then looked up at her father and gave him a weak smile. "No, thank you." How could she ever explain what she was doing back there in the woods? How was she ever going to erase that gruesome image from her memory? How could she face all the questions she'd get from the kids at school?

Isaac filled Claudia in on the relatively few, but certainly concerning, details he knew about Avery's traumatic experience, and while Claudia comforted her and hoped to get the rest of the story of the events of the day, they thought it wise for Isaac to alert Edna, their cleaning lady and dear friend, of the situation.

Isaac made the short trip to St. Louis Park and turned into the driveway in front of the little yellow Cape Cod. There she was on her hands and knees, digging in the garden. Isaac put the car in park and readied himself to deliver the news. Undeniably, if it hadn't been for Crystal Holt's murder, he wouldn't even know Edna. And what a blessing she was.

Upon hearing his arrival, Edna sat back on her shins and looked toward the drive. A big smile erupted causing a starburst of wrinkles around her eyes. "Detective! What a surprise."

He waved at the little sprite of a woman. "Edna, don't you ever stop?"

"Now why would I want to do that? If I stopped, I might not start again."

Isaac couldn't help but smile. Even though she was closing in on eighty, Edna had more get up and go than a toddler.

"No," she said. "I prefer to be the one planting the daisies, not the one pushing 'em up, you know."

How apropos, Isaac thought, considering the subject matter of the day. It hadn't taken long for Cynthia to confirm that the cadaver was indeed Garrett Holt.

"Don't you just love the spring, Detective?"

She still insisted on calling him Detective even after their relationship had changed from victim/detective to employee/employer. "I do," he agreed.

"All this beauty sprouting up all 'round? I declare! Just look at these poppies – bigger than my hand!" She held her open hand next to one of the flowers for comparison.

"Indeed they are."

Her bright blue eyes twinkled. "Now come on over here and help me up."

"Happy to, Edna." Isaac walked over and stood ready to do as requested.

Edna pulled off her pink gardening gloves and tucked them in the pocket of her gardening apron. She rose to her knees and rolled her toes under. Isaac held out both hands, she placed hers in his and stood. At full height, she stood just under five feet. Dirt and grass clumps stuck to her knees.

"You know, I'll be cleaning your house tomorrow," she said. She adjusted the spectacles on her face and squinted up at him. "'Lest you're here to fire me, that is."

Isaac chuckled at the ludicrous statement. "Edna, we'd be lost without you. You're part of the family now."

She patted his arm. "Well, aren't you as sweet as honey. Never 'spected to be adopted at my age. But very grateful for it!"

A rustle in the bushes caught their attention and a fury black head popped out from under the hedge.

"Looky there," Edna said. "Eb's comin' out to see you."

The cat walked over and started weaving between Isaac's legs.

"He must recognize your voice." She bent forward and brushed the dirt off her pant legs. "Animals have that instinct, you know. They know who they can trust. Go ahead now, Detective," she urged. "Pick him up."

Isaac lifted the cat and he snuggled into Isaac's arms. "Hey, Ebony," he said. "Look's like Edna's taking good care of you."

"Lordy be!" she exclaimed. "Listen to that cat purr! Just as loud as my daddy's old Hudson."

It was only three months ago Isaac had held this cat after the death of Crystal Holt, Ebony's former owner, and Edna's former employer. Only three months ago Crystal was found dead with a gunshot wound to the head, and Edna was laid out cold in the hallway after being struck from behind with an iron skillet. A few days later, Garrett Holt disappeared, Edna adopted Ebony, and Isaac and family adopted Edna – originally as their housekeeper, but she was now forever in their hearts.

Edna watched as Isaac gave Eb a gentle kiss on the head. She could sense something was wrong. "So, what brings you 'round here, Detective?"

He pursed his lips, not sure how to begin. "I've got some news, Edna."

"Go on," she encouraged.

"We found Garrett Holt." *"We" wasn't exactly correct.*

Edna nodded. Was he worried this news would scare her in some way? "Well, I'm glad for it. Where did that good-for-nothing scallywag get off to, anyway? It's about time he come back and settle everything. That house has sat empty for nearly three months. I shiver to think of all the critters that may have moved in by now." She wagged her pointer finger back and forth. "He better not come lookin' to me to get it all spruced up."

A squirrel darted past catching Ebony's attention. Ebony leapt from Isaac's grasp after it. The squirrel ran up a nearby tree and Ebony howled at it from below.

"Eb, you come away from there and leave that poor squirrel alone," Edna scolded. She extended Isaac's arm and inspected the scratch Ebony had left behind. "Oh pooh!" she said, and pulled out a spray bottle from her apron. "So sorry, Detective. That Eb is just a little dickens." She squirted some water on Isaac's arm, then took out a clean paper towel and patted Isaac's injury.

Other men may have pulled away and objected to this, but Isaac knew that was pointless. Edna would insist, so he'd learned it was best to just allow it.

"There now. That should heal right up."

The squirrel skipped effortlessly across the tree branches onto a neighboring tree. Eb dropped low to the ground and stealthily crept along after him.

"Thanks, Edna. You always take such good care of me."

"Well, that's what the good Lord put me here on earth to do." She stuffed the towel back into her pocket and adjusted the spectacles on her face. "So what's the scuttlebutt about Garrett?"

Isaac set his hand on her shoulder. "Edna, Garrett's dead."

"Dead?"

"Yes."

She bowed her head. "God rest his soul," she said. And then she frowned. "It was all his fault Crystal was killed, you know."

Even though Garrett Holt wasn't the one to actually pull the trigger, Isaac thought there was some truth to that statement.

"And Lord knows I've tried, but I still haven't been able to forgive him for that. You know he didn't even attend her funeral?"

Isaac was quite aware of that, especially since Garrett had disappeared after their first interview and the police had been hoping to catch up with him at that exact event. Of course, now they knew that even if Garrett had wanted to, he wouldn't have been able. "He was probably dead before then."

"Really? So, how'd he die?"

"He was shot."

Edna nodded "So, they got him," she said.

"They?"

"The mob or whoever he consorted with. You know, he'd leave the house and never tell Crystal where he was off to. But we all suspected. Why else would he be needing all that money all the time?" She shook her head in disgust. "Where did you find him?"

Here was the news he didn't want to share. But Edna needed to know before she came to the house. She needed to understand what was going on. "He was found in the woods of Birchwood Park this morning." Isaac rubbed his forehead. "Actually, Edna. It was Avery who found him."

Her hands flew to her cheeks. "Oh, heaven help us. That poor child."

CHAPTER 7

Nikki heard the whine of the garage door opening and jumped up from her chair. Tucker was home. She looked at the clock. Five thirty on the dot. As always.

She pulled the T-shirt over her head and tossed it into the laundry room as she made a beeline for the bathroom down the hall. She slipped her arms into the brand-new Diane von Fürstenberg wrap and pulled the fabric belt from the right side through the button hole opening at the waist, took the fabric belt piece from the left, crossed them behind her back, and tied them together in front. She reached in and adjusted her breasts in the demurely sexy frock, showing them off to their full advantage.

She heard the back door open.

She picked up the lipstick and applied it to her ample lips. Her best feature, she had been told. She pressed them together to spread the pale pink shade evenly.

Tucker's keys landed in the ceramic bowl by the entry with a clang.

She took the comb to her pert pixie cut, letting the bangs fall across her forehead, and then stepped into a pair of Valentino flats. There would be no spikes tonight — on the top or the bottom. She took a final assessment in the mirror. Tinkerbell without the bun. Perfect.

She heard Tucker open the refrigerator door, just as he always did. She was amazed how his routine never varied. Like clockwork. It was so easy to predict. So dependable.

She entered the kitchen as he popped the top on his beer. He wasn't much to look at with his bulging eyes and increasingly bulging belly. "Hey hot stuff," she said.

He pushed his horn-rimmed glasses back up the sharp slope of his nose with his middle finger. "Wow. Look at you." He hadn't seen her in a dress since the last fundraising event they had forced her to attend. He knew she preferred yoga pants, shorts and tight T-shirts. In fact, the way she looked in a tight T-shirt was one of the things that first drew him to her. But that was another time. Another place.

She saw his eyes light up. Just the way they used to. "It's new. I thought you'd like it."

He took a gulp of beer and licked his thin lips. "Very nice."

"Befitting a representative's wife?"

"Definitely. Is it for a particular occasion?"

She clasped her hands together like little girls do. "Thought you might take me to dinner. I missed you last weekend."

Missed him? Was that true? Nevertheless, it would definitely be good for them to be seen in public together enjoying themselves. Particularly since there had been whispers of trouble between them. He'd like nothing more than to squelch that. Make it appear that things were never better. And amazingly, the timing was perfect. He felt like he had been handed a gift on a silver platter. "That's a great idea."

She smiled. She had always been a good fisherman. All it took was the right lure and a little jiggle on the line. She knew full well this outing would be good for him, but it would also be good for her.

He set the beer on the counter. "I'll just go freshen up."

She watched him stride down the hall to the bedroom. When the bedroom door closed, she moved in slowly to listen.

Tucker pulled his phone out of his coat pocket. Of course, now that he had officially thrown his hat into the ring, all these things needed to go through the proper channels and be approved. This proved to be much more constraining than he had imagined. He felt much like a puppet, but fortunately, he'd managed to find a few ways to escape the constant scrutiny and pull his own strings.

He touched the number and heard it ringing.

"What's up?" asked the voice at the other end of the line.

"Perry, I'd like to take my wife out to dinner."

"Your wife? Are you sure?"

"Yes," Tucker said indignantly. "Would I call if I wasn't? Where can we go to get the most exposure?"

"Tuck, this doesn't sound like a good idea. You know we need to *limit* her exposure."

"But she looks great tonight. Believe me, tonight would be a very good night for exposure."

Perry ran his hand over his face. How many times had they talked about this? Having her on Tucker's resume looked good to the voters, but letting her out in public was a crap shoot. "I'm sorry, Tuck, but she's a time bomb."

"I know, I know, Perry." *That's what they all said.* "But I disagree. I think this would be good for us."

"Tuck, do I need to remind you what happened at Crooners?"

"No, but this will be different. I promise."

"Are you sure?"

"Yes." *It was always better when it was just the two of them.* He could keep her in line.

"We've discussed this. Your father won't be happy."

Here we go again. Would he ever be seen as more than just his father's son? He felt the ire rise on the back of his neck. But he'd show them all soon enough. He had his own strategic plan for the election. He'd be a shoo-in. "He'll get over it," he said petulantly. "This will be good for us. Good for the campaign."

Perry sighed. Tucker wasn't giving up and Perry knew how peevish Tucker could be when he didn't get his way. *Would he ever grow up?* If he didn't pacify him, they'd be at this all night. "Okay, you know what?" he said. "Let's arrange something for next week."

"No, not next week," Tucker barked. "Tonight," he said emphatically. "I want to take my wife out TO-NIGHT."

Nikki smiled on the other side of the door. Tucker could get quite prickly when he didn't get his way. She had counted on it.

Perry pursed his lips. "Okay. Let me see what I can come up with."

A few minutes later, the phone rang. "Yeah?" Tuck said.

"I got you a table at the Dakota."

"Perfect. You won't regret this."

"You're going to make sure I don't."

♦♦♦

The maître d' sat them at a table just to the right of the stage.

"Great table," Nikki said as Tucker pulled the chair out for her.

Surely, everyone else in the establishment had ordered their show tickets in advance, but if the Rennickes wanted a table, they usually got one.

Nikki sat and Tucker gave her a loving peck on the top of her head for all to see.

She smiled up at him.

Tucker pushed his horn-rimmed glasses back up his nose with his middle finger and took a seat in the chair next to her.

The waiter arrived and handed them each a menu. "The show will begin in fifteen minutes. May I get you a beverage while you look at the menu?"

"Yes. Thank you," Tucker said to the waiter using the stilted, official representative's voice he used in public.

Nikki internally rolled her eyes while keeping a smile glued to her face. How she hated that ridiculous voice.

"I'll have a Manhattan and my lovely wife would like a Moscato." Tucker smiled endearingly at Nikki. "Right, honey?"

She nodded. "That would be lovely." *Yeah, that would be lovely for your mother*, she thought to herself. She had never liked sweet wine and would have much preferred a whiskey sour, but Tucker had never been all that interested in what she wanted, just in how she looked – more particularly, how she looked to others, and most importantly, how she made *him* look. But, the point of tonight was to try to get along. So, get along she would.

Once the waiter was gone, Nikki took Tucker's hand. Just like she used to. "Let's go north this weekend," she said.

He leaned back in his chair. "I was just there."

A sound technician tapped the microphone center stage.

"But not with me." She clasped his hand in both of hers. "Doesn't it sound good for us to get away together? Just you and me?"

She was right. That certainly did sound good. The happy couple with plans for a romantic weekend in Greater Minnesota. Just another tidbit to help put an end to the rumors they were discontented. "Yes," Tucker agreed. "It sounds perfect."

The waiter returned with the drinks and set them on the table. "I'll give you a chance to look through the menu and then I'll stop back," he said.

"Thank you," Tucker responded.

Nikki pushed her wine to the side. "We could go to your folk's cabin. Daddy could get it opened for us."

Tucker held up his glass in a toast. "Yes. Absolutely. Let's."

Nikki set her elbows on the table and leaned in. "When can we leave?"

"We'll have to go on Saturday." He swirled the liquid around in his glass. "I have a meeting on Friday."

"A meeting? All day?"

"Yes." He pushed his glasses in place and picked up the menu. "It's hard to say how long it will take. And afterwards, I'll have to be around as things . . . develop."

Develop? Whatever that meant, she wasn't going to let it derail their trip. It was far too important to her. "Okay."

Tucker folded the menu, took another drink and licked his lips.

Some roadies brought out a couple guitars and placed them in stands in front of the drum kit.

Nikki stuck out her bottom lip. "Then I won't cancel with Hans."

"You have an appointment with Hans?" How he despised Hans with his fake name, fake accent, bleached hair and washboard stomach. Tucker was sure that Hans' interest in Nikki went beyond that of a personal trainer, and he suspected there was much more to their relationship than just fitness. But still, she shouldn't cancel. It wouldn't look good if she canceled.

She picked up her menu. "Yeah, Friday night is hot yoga," she said.

"*Hot* yoga?"

Her eyes sparkled. "Oh, yes. *Very* hot yoga."

Tucker felt suddenly warm and his neck turned crimson. It surprised him how the jealousy still took hold of him.

Nikki wet her lips and let out a loud whistle as the band members took the stage.

CHAPTER 8

Isaac sat at the table glassy eyed, with the file in front of him. Since they had solved Crystal Holt's murder back in February, Garrett's disappearance hadn't been anything worth looking into at the time. After all, Garrett hadn't been charged with any crime and no one had officially reported him missing. For all they knew, he could have gone on vacation. But, now that they had a body, they would have to revisit all they knew, retrace their steps, and find out who had a motive to kill Mr. Garrett Holt.

"You look tired, Jefe," Tom said.

"Haven't gotten much sleep over the last couple days," Isaac responded. Partly because of Avery's nightly nightmares, and partly just out of worry. They were told by the counselor that individuals who have experienced trauma often need to regain a feeling of safety, so they were doing their best to make Avery feel safe. Exactly how that was different than the way they lived before, Isaac couldn't really say. He had finally concluded that it wasn't *different*, it was just more concentrated. Like frozen orange juice. Essentially the same, but without the fluidity.

"How's Avery doing?"

"Okay." Isaac ran his hand over his face. "She seems fine one minute, then cries if her peas touch the meat on her plate." He sighed. "And she snapped at Isabelle for leaving her Barbie in the bathroom yesterday." He shook his head. "She's just not quite herself."

He had no plans of sharing, but Tom knew what it was like to experience psychological stress. He could relate to Avery. The best analogy he heard during his recovery was that one who is emotionally overwhelmed is like a shaken bottle of soda. Inside the bottle there is a tremendous amount of pressure and the safest way to release that pressure is to open and close the cap in a slow, deliberate manner so as to prevent an explosion. "She just needs to let off some steam," Tom said. "Little by little," he added. "It will just take time."

"Yeah." Isaac sighed again. "She's going back to school today." He hoped it was because she felt stronger, and not because she wanted to see John Rogers. He couldn't help but wonder what she was doing back in the woods with him. A father's biggest worry for their daughters was that their innocence would be shattered by some uncaring cad. He'd certainly need to talk with Avery about it, but not just yet.

"Getting back to the routine will be good for her."

Isaac nodded. "I hope so."

Just then, Red popped his head in the door. Red wasn't his real name, but it seemed only natural to call him that given his bright red locks. "Got some more stuff here." He dropped the file on the table getting them back to the business at hand.

Isaac reached for it. If anyone knew about Garrett Holt, Red did. Red had tailed Garrett to the casino right after he had been to the morgue to identify his dead wife, and he had also tailed Garrett to the coffee shop he visited just before he disappeared.

"Thanks, Red," Isaac said. "Take a seat. Petruco should be here any minute."

Red felt a shiver go up his spine. The last person he wanted to see was Captain Petruco. This case had haunted him for the last three months. Fortunately, they caught Garrett's wife's murderer, but Red still kicked himself for letting Garrett slip away. His job had been to follow Garrett and keep him under surveillance, and he had failed – and Petruco was not letting him forget it.

As Red sat down, Captain Petruco entered the room. The captain was swarthy, had close-set eyes, and walked with his shoulders hunched forward giving him the look of a vulture. He stopped just inside the door. His sharp beaklike nose moved from one face to the next. "Where's Vick?" he asked.

"Remember? Vick moved to California last week," Isaac said.

"Oh yeah. Smart move." He zeroed in on Tom. "Who's he?"

"This is Tom Bryant, my new partner. He's taking Vick's place."

Tom stood to shake Petruco's hand.

"He's from Wisconsin," Isaac added.

Why everyone felt they needed to say that he was from Wisconsin dumbfounded Tom. "Green Bay," Tom said. "The home of the Packers." Actually, Tom was from Milwaukee, but he now knew that nothing got Minnesotans more worked up than the mention of the Packers.

"The Packers suck," Petruco said.

"The Packers win," Tom retorted.

Petruco cackled at that. "I like him," he said to Isaac. "He's got spunk." Petruco gave a wave to Tom as an instruction to sit down and sat across from Isaac. "What do we got?"

"A lot of guesswork as always, Captain. It looks like someone nabbed him from the coffee shop," Isaac said.

"We already thought that, didn't we?" Petruco pointed his boney finger at Red. "You should have followed him. If you had followed him, we wouldn't be in this mess."

"I was undercover," Red answered. He ran his hands nervously through his red mane. "I didn't want him to know he was being watched. If I had followed him, that would have been a dead give-away."

"Well that's exactly what it was." Petruco slammed his palms on the table. "You gave him away and now he's dead."

"I thought he went to the bathroom," Red explained for the umpteenth time. "That's what the sign above the door said." Unknown to Red at the time, the door opened into a hallway with shared lavatory facilities for the businesses in the strip mall, but it was also an exit to the back alley.

Petruco threw up his hands. "And now we get to try to find out who killed him three months later. Three months later," Petruco repeated loudly. "After the trail has gone cold."

♦♦♦

Claudia pulled her car into the school parking lot. Understandably, Avery didn't want to take the bus today. She said she wasn't ready for that yet. But Claudia wondered if she was ready for school at all. Avery hadn't had more than a few hours of fitful sleep at a time since returning home on Saturday and her emotions were all out of kilter. "You can call me anytime and I'll come get you," she said to Avery.

"Thanks, Mom. But I'll be okay." Avery had stayed home on Monday not ready to deal with all the questions that were sure to come her way about the events of the weekend, but judging by the number of texts and calls she had received, she couldn't put it off any longer. Their discovery had been the top news story all weekend. And even though the police had done their best to protect their identities, the news crews managed to snap a few photos. And even though the press had blurred out their faces since they were minors, it wasn't hard for those who knew them to figure out who they were. Word spread like wildfire and the rumors had started to get out of control. So, after a good cry, Avery decided to go in and put this all behind her. *How bad could it be?* Sure, she'd get bombarded with questions, but once they got that out of their systems, she hoped to get support and understanding from her classmates. She stepped out of the SUV and secured her back pack on her shoulder with resolve.

"Love you, honey," Claudia said.

"Love you too, Mom."

Claudia watched her walk past the buses and throngs of children to the front entry. Her heart went out to her first born. She remembered the day she and Isaac brought Avery home from the hospital and what a surprising adjustment it had been. From that moment on, they were continually adjusting and adapting as Avery continually grew, adapted and adjusted. Each month, each year, brought new challenges, new surprises. But this latest event was one surprise Claudia had never considered. How was Avery to get past it? As an infant, she was strong willed and persistent. She didn't cry when things didn't go her way, she just kept trying. She walked at ten months, she could write her name at age three, and she was now a straight A student. Claudia hoped Avery would bring that same confidence and tenacity with her today. Because she knew from personal experience just how thoughtless and downright mean children could be. Especially at this age.

Claire, Avery's best friend since kindergarten, stood waiting for her inside the vestibule. "Hey," she said in greeting.

"Hey," Avery responded.

"You won't believe what those creepy boys are doing," Claire warned. She thought it would be best to give Avery the heads-up before she saw it for herself. But as they opened the foyer door, it was already too late.

A group of boys from the basketball team jerked by in zombie fashion with their arms stretched out in front making zombie-like groans and grunts. Avery and Claire watched them pass. "Idiots," Claire said.

Avery glanced over and saw John Rogers at his locker just down the hall. Because of his height, she spotted him easily in the throng of students. The hair on the back of her neck rose up and her stomach churned. *How had she been so stupid?*

She watched the boys continue down the hall, straight-legged, toward him.

Upon seeing them, John Rogers threw his head back and laughed. "I always knew you guys were nothing but dead weight." Of course, he'd never tell them about the nightmares that were invading his sleep, or how he'd taken to leaving the light on at night, or how he broke into tears when he dropped ketchup on his favorite football jersey. Only the ever-darker bags under his eyes and the twitch that had developed at the corner of his mouth would give that away.

"Boys are so dumb," Claire said.

Avery couldn't have agreed more.

Claire grabbed Avery's arm. "Com'mon, let's go." She pulled her away from the spectacle.

As they made their way through the sea of students filing down the hallway, Avery heard kissy noises as they passed. She didn't turn to see who made them, but noticed Claire shot them a dirty look. The puckering paused for a moment, but then the kids giggled and started in again.

Avery felt mortified. *What had he told them? Did everyone know?*

Thankfully Avery arrived to her destination, and, with a sigh of relief, took her usual seat in first period English. She looked up at the clock on the wall. *This was going to be a long day.* As she pulled out her book, she felt a tap on her shoulder. She set her book on her desk and turned around.

"I didn't know your dad was a cop," Gina said.

She'd known Gina for over three years now. While they weren't close friends, they hung out with the same crowd. "Oh, yeah. He is," Avery responded. "A detective."

"Oooh! Watch out!" Gina said and held her hands up like she was under arrest.

"Funny," Avery said and turned back around. She felt her temperature rising. Actually, she didn't think it was funny at all. *I mean, who cares what your classmate's parents do for a living?* She stewed about it some more and tapped her pencil against the desktop. Unless, it seemed, they happened to be a cop.

When first period ended, Avery set off quickly toward her locker, feeling like the eyes of the world were on her, as if a spot light followed her every movement.

A group of boys looked up as she drew near. "Stay away from that one," one of them said, "or you might end up in the clink." They all got a good chuckle out of that.

Tears stung her eyes. She picked up her pace. As she moved faster, the hurt turned to anger while unsettling questions spun through her head. *What had that conceited liar told everyone? How could he be so cruel? How could she have been so stupid?* Well, she'd make sure the truth was told.

Avery arrived at her locker and found Jessica waiting there. She looked like the green-eyed monster itself.

Jessica pointed her finger in Avery's face. "You stay away from John Rogers, Avery Scott."

This was the encounter Avery had been dreading the most. But now surprisingly, it would be the easiest to handle. "Hey Jessica, no problem there," she assured her. "I want nothing to do with him."

Jessica put her hands on her hips and stuck out her bottom lip. "Oh yeah? Then what were you doing with him in the woods?"

Avery raised her eyebrows. "Well, certainly not what I've heard you do with him."

Jessica gasped, turned from green to bright red, and stomped off.

CHAPTER 9

Glen pounded his meaty fist against the door with all his might. Not surprisingly, the two-hour drive to get here from Plummer's Point had only served to increase his anger. The apartment number, which had once been a nine, but since the loss of its upper nail was now a six, swung back and forth as the door shook with each impact. "Richie!" he called. "Open this door!"

Silence.

He pulled, and turned, and rattled the knob, but to no avail. "Richie!"

No response.

He put his ear against the door. "I know you're in there, Richie!"

Still no answer.

He kicked the door in frustration. "Damn it, Richie. Open up!" He looked up and down the drab hallway. Two bulbs were broken in the ceiling lamps making it harder to see the filthy, worn carpeting that had probably been there since the turn of the century.

He tried to peer through the eyehole. "You better be dead in there, kid, or I'm gonna kill you."

He heard a dull thud against the other side of the door. "Who is it?" came a voice from the other side.

"You know damn well who it is, son. Now open up."

The door opened a crack, the chain link preventing further movement.

Richie yawned, looking like he just rolled out of bed. "Okay, okay. Just calm down. What's up?"

"You stole my truck!"

Richie sighed and scratched the back of his head further messing up his snarled hair. "No, no. I didn't steal it."

Glen's face turned a bright red. "I see it in the parking lot." He pointed forcefully down the hallway toward the entry of the apartment building. "It's right there. Now how did it get there if you didn't steal it?"

"Chill out." Richie stretched his right arm over his head and leaned to the left. "I didn't steal it, I borrowed it."

"Borrowed it?" Glen exclaimed.

The door across the hall opened and a woman peeked out. "Keep it down." She pointed her finger through the opening. "I'm warning you, Richie. I'll call the cops one of these days."

"I know, I know," Richie responded. "We'll be quiet now." He gave Glen a stern look. "Oh, and thanks for the sugar cookies, Mrs. Kilbernie. Nobody makes 'em like you do."

"Glad you liked them, Richie." She put her pointer finger to her lips and then shook it at Glen. "Quiet down now you." She closed her door and they heard the lock turn.

"Borrowed it?" Glen repeated more quietly this time, but the venom still oozed from his lips. "I don't think so. Borrowing usually involves asking, and you never asked me."

Richie shrugged. "Mine wouldn't start, so I took yours."

"Without asking?" Glen shouted.

"Shhhh," Richie warned. "Geez, can't you say anything without yelling?" He held up his palm. "Just hold on. I'll let you in."

Richie closed the door, unlatched the chain lock, then opened it for Glen to enter into the small, efficiency apartment. It was furnished with hand-me-downs, Goodwill purchases and a few pieces Glen figured must have been pulled from the dumpster. His mother's old sheets covered the windows. A kitchen table doubled as a TV stand. Richie's grandmother's walnut coffee table sported an overflowing ashtray and a variety of remotes.

"I didn't want to wake you," Richie said. "Besides, you have other vehicles. Hell, the shop is full of vehicles. It's no big deal."

"It's a very big deal, son. You can't just take things without asking."

"Stop calling me son. You're not my father."

Glen pounded his chest. "I raised you and without me you'd just be another bastard child."

Richie walked over and collapsed on a well-worn sofa that doubled as his bed. "Mom raised me." He crossed his arms over his chest.

"And you're killing her!"

"Oh, stop with the dramatics."

Glen started to pace. "She's worried sick about you. And I'm worried sick about her. This shit has got to stop. This is the last straw." He stopped and narrowed his eyes. "Now give me the keys."

"No can do."

"I said, give me the keys!"

"Man, really, just calm down. No worries. I'll bring it back this weekend. I got a job and I need transportation."

"A job?"

"Yeah, that's what you want right?"

Glen looked at him skeptically. "If you're playing me, kid, I'll call the cops on you. I swear it this time."

Richie knew that would never happen. His mother would be beside herself. "Honest truth."

"What kind of job?"

"Can't tell."

Glen let out a snort. "No, no, no you don't. Do you think I'm stupid? Don't you think I know what this smell is?" He held out his arms and sniffed in with his nose. "If you're thinking you're going to use my truck for some kind of drug deal, you're wrong, buster."

"No drug deal."

"History would say otherwise." *How many times had Sheriff Nilsson showed up at his house with Richie by his side?* He could have arrested him, but in the small town of Plummer's Point, thankfully, the Sheriff practiced leniency and compassion for the residents.

"It's not a drug deal."

Glen threw his hands to his head as if it would burst if he didn't hold it together. "Who are you messing around with, Richie? You do know that people will use you."

"I said don't worry. I'll bring your stupid truck back."

That was it. "Damn it, Richie!" Glen lunged toward him, but Richie jumped up from the couch and twisted away. Glen kept steadily after him. "Don't give me the run around, boy. If this was a real job you could tell me."

Richie ducked around the back of the sofa and tripped over the suitcase he had set there just the day before. He landed on his rear and held up his hands in self-defense. "Fine. Fine," he said. "Don't have a heart attack. Just chill. I'll tell you."

Glen stood over him, waiting.

"It's a job for the Rennickes."

"The Rennickes?"

Richie knew that would get his attention. Glen's hatred for that family ran deep and had been impossible to hide, try as he might. "Yeah. Real hush hush, so you can't say a word to anyone. Ever."

"Why would the Rennickes call you?"

"Remember Tuck?"

He remembered Tuck, the stuck-up spoiled prick. He had also heard the stuck-up spoiled prick was running for office, following in his unscrupulous father's footsteps. "That little snot nose brat?"

"Yep. That's the one."

Could he believe him?

"But seriously, no one can know. Tuck would kill me if he found out I told you."

Glen backed off. "You know I don't talk to those people." And it certainly got his ire up that Richie did.

Richie shoved the suitcase out of the way and stood.

Glen noticed the Macy's price tag. "What's that?"

Richie shrugged. "I'm moving out of here."

Moving out? "You said you had a job."

"Yeah, yeah. Because of the job."

"Where are you going?"

"I don't know where *specifically*." He picked up the bag and placed it next to the couch. "Someplace else – a better place. Like I said, Glen. No worries. All's good."

How his mother hated it when Richie called him Glen. And how Glen hated to see his wife torn apart between them. "You better not be pulling my leg, kid. I mean it this time."

CHAPTER 10

Ah, a perfect seventy-eight degree day. Isaac stood at the railing on the deck and looked out over the backyard. A light breeze blew across his face and the fragrance of freshly mowed grass filled his nostrils. A flock of Canada geese, returning to Minnesota waters after a long winter, honked overhead as they switched leaders in their traveling V. Isabelle was swinging from the playset without a care in the world. Avery was inside working on homework and returning to her good-natured self. Jacob was at basketball practice. Isaac took a deep breath. At just that moment, life felt very good.

Claudia came up next to him holding two glasses of wine. "Here you go," she said, and handed one to him.

He held up his glass. "To my beautiful wife." What would he do without her? She was the glue that held them all together. Why Tom wasn't out looking for this, he'd never understand. But Tom just kept saying that he had no desire to go on endless dates chasing after women; that when the right one came along, he'd know it. Isaac knew it certainly had been that way for him. The moment he saw Claudia, his whole life focus changed. They each took a sip. "How's it going for Avery at school?"

"She's quite tight-lipped about it." In fact, when asked, all she ever said to them was that she didn't want to talk about it. "I could tell Tuesday was difficult at school, but each day since seems better."

The nightmares had lessened as well, so they were all getting caught up on lost sleep. It had been days since she last burst into tears, and she actually laughed out loud at Jacob's tale of the gym teacher that fell into the pool during his afternoon class. But Avery's appetite was non-existent. At dinner, she just pushed the food around her plate. In the evening, she sat in front of the television with Walter, who for the time being, was allowed on the couch as long as he stayed on the blanket Edna put there to protect it. Avery and Walter were developing quite a bond and Claudia was beginning to wonder if Avery would insist this bending of the rules become permanent.

Still, they hadn't been able to get any details of Avery's exploration in the woods with John Rogers, but they weren't ready to push. They hoped Edna was right and that time would heal all.

They watched as Isabelle, their sprightly five-year-old, true blessing, and pleasant surprise of their love, conceived years after they thought their family was complete, leapt off the swing, landed soundly on the grass, and then ran around and climbed up the ladder on the side of the wooden playset. Once she reached the top platform, she began singing "How Far I'll Go," from her favorite movie, *Moana*. Isaac reached out and grasped Claudia's hand while they watched as she danced and twirled around with theatric flair. Their Isabelle, a bright light of energy, without whom all of them, including ten-year-old Jacob and thirteen-year-old Avery, would be the lessor. For the big finale, she spun around the post and slid down the slide.

Isaac and Claudia applauded. Isabelle took a bow, then ran off to continue playing.

Claudia pulled up a stool. "How's the investigation going?"

Isaac sipped his wine. "Slow. We've got the crew scouring the area for clues and so far we've come up with a gum wrapper, a broken piece of jewelry, some old soda pop cans, some cigarette butts and more junk like that." Forensics would do what they could with them, but at this point they had no good leads.

"One of those may break the case wide open."

"Let's hope so." Isaac took a seat on the stool to her left. "Red has been undercover getting the word on the street. He says the bookies were livid upon learning Garrett had been killed. They thought he'd skipped town. They've had people searching for Garrett for months now. He was a steady source of income for them—with very deep pockets."

Isabelle slid down the slide with a shout of glee, then ran around to climb the ladder again as the sun began its descent casting a mix of pink and orange across the sky.

"Speaking of deep pockets," Claudia said. "Guess who stopped by the office today?"

"Who?"

"Edna."

"Edna? Was she downtown shopping?"

Claudia took a sip of her wine. "No, not shopping. She had an appointment with Crystal Holt's attorney. Now that they have confirmation Garrett is dead, they can complete the distribution of Crystal's *massive* estate."

"So what does that have to do with Edna?"

Isabelle shrieked causing them both to jerk their heads in her direction.

Claudia stood to get a better look. "Isabelle, are you okay?"

"I'm a monkey!" Isabelle said happily, and grasped the bar between the swings.

"Yes, you are!" Claudia exclaimed as she returned to her seat.

"I thought Edna already received her inheritance," Isaac said. And, it was quite a hefty sum as Isaac recalled.

So large in fact, they often wondered why she still came to work for them.

"Yes, that's right. All the distributions were made after Crystal's death according to her will, but the balance of the money has been held in trust for Garrett. Now that he's gone, that money needs to be distributed according to the trust."

"And Edna gets a part of that?"

Claudia nodded. "Oh, yes."

Isaac raised his brows. "Really."

"Do you remember Crystal's parents were killed in a car crash and Crystal, the sole heir, inherited their millions?"

Of course he did. Everyone initially assumed that money was the motive for Crystal's murder. "Yes."

"Well, with no parents, I understand that Crystal looked to Edna as a mother figure." Claudia smiled. "And because of that, Crystal wanted to be sure Edna was taken care of."

Isaac scooted toward the edge of his seat to be sure he was hearing her properly.

Claudia's smile grew wider. "I don't know the amount, but our Edna will soon be a very wealthy lady."

"Ha!" Isaac exclaimed. "Well I couldn't be happier for her."

"How does it feel knowing our housekeeper has more money than we'll ever have?"

CHAPTER 11

Nikki pulled the bags down from the garage shelf. She wanted to be absolutely sure everything was ready. She was determined not to let anything get in the way of their trip to Plummer's Point. The way things were going right now, it could be her saving grace. *What had Tucker said? He had to be around to see how things developed?* Well, she wasn't going to let him weasel out of it. He could be so petulant. But then, she knew Tucker better than he knew himself. Come hell or high water she'd get him in that car.

She reviewed her checklist. She tapped her newly polished nails on the granite countertop. Just one more thing needed to be done. She picked up her cell and dialed.

The phone was answered on the second ring. "Sheriff Nilsson."

"Hi Daddy," Nikki said.

"Nikki!" The Sheriff exclaimed, then settled back in his chair. She rarely called anymore, so he figured she must need something. "What's up?"

"Wondering if you could open the Rennicke's cabin this weekend?"

"Of course. Are you finally leaving that rich, sissy citiot and coming home where you belong?" How she ended up with Tucker Rennicke, he'd never understand.

She laughed, but this had always been a point of contention between them. He'd practically refused to walk her down the aisle. "Oh stop it, Daddy."

"You're too good for him."

Here we go again. "I know."

"He doesn't treat you well."

Same speech as always. "I know."

"And don't even get me started on his family."

But Nikki was sure that her father's issues with the family would pale in comparison to hers.

♦♦♦

It had all started the summer before her junior year of high school. The summer Nikki decided to insert herself into their world. Her plan was a simple one. First, she stopped by the local gift shop and picked up a butterfly net and field guide. Then she went home, took one of the Skippy jars she'd been saving all winter, and pounded a nail over and over in the lid to make air holes. She tied a string around the jar, attached it to her belt loop, tucked the field guide in her pocket, picked up the butterfly net and headed off on her mission.

Wearing her best shorts and the hot pink T-shirt that showed off her figure, she walked down the dirt road that led to the Rennicke's cabin. The Rennicke's had owned the twenty-acre parcel with 3,000 feet of shoreline on Lake Washburn for generations. The elder Rennicke, now Senator Rennicke, spent his boyhood summers there, as had his father and his father's father. And, following tradition, this next generation of Rennicke children spent a good amount of their summer there as well.

The original cabin was a cabin like most others, but after the death of grandfather Rennicke, Senator Rennicke razed the original structure and built a new one. It was unlike any in the area, and substantially nicer than all of the homes of the local residents. The walls were Lodgepole pine and the towering two-story windows offered a spectacular view of the lake.

Her father called it an eyesore that interrupted the beauty of the natural landscape. Nikki thought it looked like a castle made for a princess, and she was determined to be Cinderella.

Nikki traveled up and down the dirt road that led to the Rennicke's property that day waiting for an opportunity to introduce herself, but had no luck. As the sun headed toward the horizon, she headed back home.

The next two days were the same. But on the third day, she caught sight of the youngest Rennicke hiking up the driveway. As planned, Nikki held up her butterfly net and ran spritely in her direction.

"What are you doing?" called the girl.

Nikki put on her best look of surprise. "Hello!" she said. "I'm catching butterflies."

"That looks like fun," the girl said. She walked over to Nikki. "My name is Felicity. What's yours?"

Felicity was a few years younger than Nikki and infinitely more naïve.

Nikki smiled. "I'm Nikki. Want to join me?"

"Yes," Felicity said enthusiastically.

Nikki handed Felicity the butterfly net. "Here, hold this, and when you see a butterfly, sneak up slowly and try to catch it in the net."

They spent over an hour together that day and actually managed to catch a Monarch and get it in the jar.

Felicity shrieked with excitement. "Can we do this again tomorrow?"

And that was the way Nikki snared her first Rennicke. Then, as a way to lure in more Rennickes, Nikki let Felicity take the butterfly home to show her family.

The next day, Nikki came back with two nets and a new Skippy jar; Felicity showed up with her mother and father.

Senator Rennicke looked Nikki up and down. He was quite concerned when Felicity came home and told the family of her escapades that afternoon. The senator had serious apprehensions about his daughter associating with the locals, so he decided he had better assess the situation himself.

"Felicity says you like to catch butterflies," he said to Nikki.

"Yes, sir," Nikki said. "It's for a science project."

The senator's ears perked up at the words "science project."

Nikki pulled the field guide out of her pocket. "I'm trying to catch as many of these as I can. When school starts, I'll present my project to the class for extra credit."

Mr. Rennicke took the field guide and flipped through the pages. "Extra credit?"

"Yes, sir."

He nodded. "I like your initiative." He pointed a finger at Felicity. "This is okay, but don't go off this road. I want you to stay close to home."

"Yes, daddy," Felicity said.

Having heard the local women going on about Mrs. Rennicke's wardrobe over the years, Nikki turned to her and said, "What an attractive outfit, Mrs. Rennicke."

She was obviously tickled by the compliment "Why, thank you!"

Mr. Rennicke took his wife by the arm. "Come on, dear." He led her down the road toward their property.

As the senator and Mrs. Rennicke walked down the driveway to the cabin, Nikki overheard her say 'What a smart young girl,' and Nikki knew she had pulled it off.

The next day, curious to get a look at the local who had been spending time with his sister, the catch Nikki had been angling for all along showed up. Tucker Rennicke.

She had seen him sneaking around the back of Glen's Gas and Garage to meet up with Richie Quiddler in the treehouse where Richie stashed his drugs, so she knew Tucker was no angel. But in this case, that was a good thing, because she also knew it would take a penchant for rebellion on his part for her plan to work.

Tucker practically started salivating at the sight of her. "So," he said. "You like to catch butterflies?"

"I do." She smiled.

He thought her full, pink lips looked like they would taste like cotton candy. He pushed his wire rimmed glasses up his nose. "So, show me."

It was the opportunity Nikki had dreamed of. She walked over to him slowly with the net up in the air.

Tucker felt a warmth course through his body as she drew near.

"Like this," she said. She put her left hand on his shoulder and stood on her toes.

Her touch made his heart race.

She set the net on top of his head and smiled. "Gotcha."

Youthful Felicity thought Nikki's little prank was hilarious and laughed loudly.

Tucker swooned. She was so close. She was so beautiful. She was so inviting. He licked his lips. He had never wanted anything more in his life.

Nikki was making good progress building a rapport with the Rennickes until Monica showed up a week later.

Monica was the eldest of the Rennicke children and had just returned from a tour of Europe. Her limo pulled up alongside Nikki and Felicity on the dirt road kicking up a cloud of dust.

"Monica!" Felicity squealed and ran to the side of the car.

Monica lowered her window.

"Welcome home!" Felicity said to her. "How was your flight?"

"Ugh! It was long and tedious, but I guess that's the price you have to pay," Monica said. "I would hardly call *that* first class. I could barely move. How anyone could make that trip in the back with the rabble is beyond me."

Nikki stepped up next to Felicity. Her eyes lit up as she viewed the interior of the limousine. "You were on a plane?"

Monica leered at Nikki. "Yes, I was on a plane. How else would one get back from Europe?" She looked to Felicity. "Who is this?"

"This is Nikki. She's from town."

Monica gave Nikki the once over. "You *live* here?"

Nikki nodded. "Yes."

"All year?"

"Yes."

"How horrible."

Nikki felt a prickling sensation at the back of her neck, but she knew a confrontation would get her nowhere, so she let it go. "You're right about that. I'd love to get on a plane someday."

Monica gasped. "You've never been on a plane? How can that be? Don't you *go* anywhere? You certainly can't stay up *here* all the time."

Nikki held her tongue. This one would be a challenge. Monica reminded Nikki of the snapping turtles who lunge at their unsuspecting victims with their powerful jaws and strong bite. And with her sour expression, she looked like one too.

Monica turned toward Felicity. "How dull is that?" She motioned with a wave. "Hop in Felicity, it's time for your country friend to get herself home."

That had been their first interaction and it went downhill from there.

The Rennicke's decided to have a welcome home party for Monica that weekend, and smitten Tucker asked Nikki to join them. It would be held at the Rennicke's cabin and many of the other rich, seasonal visitors would be in attendance.

Nikki spent the entire day getting ready for the event. She painted her nails, curled her hair, and put on her best dress. While the party was officially for Monica, Nikki considered it to be her social debut.

Monica greeted Nikki at the door and looked her up and down. "Nikki. How nice of you to come."

"Thank you."

Monica turned and pointed toward the back of the house. "The kitchen is down the hall. Glad you could help out."

"Ah, no," Nikki stammered. "I'm not the help. Tucker invited me."

"Oh? You're a guest?" Monica made a face. "And that's what you're wearing?"

That comment stuck in Nikki's craw all evening, but she did her best to shake it, determined to find a way into Monica's good graces. So, when Monica began regaling the group with tales about her time in London, Nikki wanted to be a part of the conversation.

Monica told of the endless flight to Heathrow, the excruciating wait in customs, the tiresome cabdriver, and the seemingly endless disappointments upon her arrival at her hotel.

"I had to wait fifteen minutes for the maître d' to get my luggage," Monica complained. "And the lift was so small, I could barely fit my bags inside."

"How awful," Nikki said, hoping her empathy would win some points. "What's a lift?"

Monica glared at her. "Don't you know anything? It's what the English call an elevator." She turned her attention to the rest of the group. "I don't think they go to school here in Plummer's Point, I think they must hibernate like the bears all winter."

Despite Monica's constant derision, Felicity still enjoyed their butterfly outings, and with the permission of her father, wanted to start a collection of her own.

The following week, Nikki brought supplies for Felicity and set them out on the side of the road. She was a bit early so she leaned back and let the sun warm her face. The purple coneflowers along the road were in full bloom and danced in the wind. Bumble bees buzzed from flower to flower sipping in their sweet nectar.

Felicity came up the driveway with her net in hand and ran off after butterflies.

Tucker followed behind and joined Nikki soaking up the sun.

"So," he said. "Want to have a campfire with me at Lake Roosevelt tonight?"

She gave him a peck on the cheek. "I'd like that."

Tucker's libido jumped into high gear. "Good." He leaned over to return the kiss, but grudgingly sat back when they heard Felicity's footsteps coming toward them across the gravel road.

"I got one! I got one!" she called.

Nikki smiled at Tucker. *So did I,* she thought to herself.

Felicity handed Nikki the net just as Monica arrived on the scene.

"What did you get?" Monica asked.

"A butterfly!" Felicity said to Monica, then turned to Nikki. "What kind is it?"

Nikki looked at the velvety dark maroon color of the body, the lacy, pale yellow edging, and the iridescent blue spots all along the border between the two. "It's a Mourning Cloak. One of my favorites."

"It's a Mourning Cloak!" Felicity repeated.

"I'm going to teach Felicity how to mount a butterfly to start her collection." Nikki told Monica.

"Did you say *teach*?"

Nikki again disregarded Monica's jab, which was becoming easier and easier with practice. "First we need to stun it, so the wings don't get damaged." Nikki held the net close around the butterfly in her left hand and put her right thumb and forefinger around the butterfly's thorax. "You squeeze here." She took her fingers away momentarily and opened the net. The butterfly didn't move.

"Cool," Tucker said.

Monica turned up her nose. "You actually touched that? How disgusting."

Nikki picked up the jar, wishing she could silence Monica as easily as she had the butterfly. She opened the lid. "This is called the killing jar," she said. "There are cotton balls soaked in rubbing alcohol in the bottom. We put the butterfly inside and close the lid. It takes about three minutes." Nikki placed the butterfly inside and began to count. "One one thousand, two one thousand, three one thousand." While she continued the counting in her head, she pulled out a square piece of foam board and a long pin from her backpack. "Then we can take it out, spread the wings, and mount it on this board."

Once they could see that the butterfly was dead, Nikki gently removed it from the jar and set it on the foam board. She spread the wings open, then took a long pin and stabbed it through the butterfly's body and into the foam board. They all heard a crackling sound as the pin went through.

"Whoa!" Tucker said.

Felicity admired the wings. "It's beautiful!"

Monica recoiled. "Ugh! How can you do that? You're like an animal."

Nikki flipped her hair back over her shoulder. "This is science, Monica," she said. "Or don't they teach that to debutantes?"

Monica's eyes turned to fire. She folded her arms across her chest. "Mother told me not to interact with the local wildlife. They might have rabies." She took her little sister's hand. "Come Felicity. Let's go."

Nikki sighed and looked over at Tucker who had picked up a beetle and thrown it in the killing jar. He held the jar in front of his face and watched the bug fly frantically around trying to make an escape. "This is awesome," he said.

She glanced past him to watch Monica and Felicity walk down to the cabin.

Monica looked back over her shoulder. "You should stay away from her," she said to Felicity.

"But Tucker likes her."

"Silly Felicity," Monica said. "Tucker would never fall for a girl like that. He's much more evolved than she is. He might play with her for a while, but then he'll release her back into the wild where she belongs."

After that, her relationship with Felicity disintegrated as Felicity started parroting her older sister's views. But all in all, Nikki was satisfied. The butterfly trap had served its purpose, and Monica was all wrong. From that time on, Tucker belonged to Nikki.

♦♦♦

"That family," her father continued.

Nikki frowned. "I know. I know." Her father was of the mind that if you repeated something enough, people would start to believe you. But in this case, he didn't need to coerce. He was spot on, on all counts. "Tell you what, when you're there opening the cabin for us, you can take your frustrations out on one of their fancy glasses or plates or something." Something she had done herself more than once, though she'd never admit it. "Will that help?"

That wasn't the remedy he was hoping for. "That would be destruction of property, young lady, and I have vowed to uphold the law. Even for citiots. So when will you arrive?"

"Saturday morning."

"I'll get it open. Will you have some time to come home and visit your old dad?"

"That's exactly why I'm coming."

He smiled. "Good. But leave Tucker at the cabin," he instructed. "I want you all to myself." That would give him a bit of private time to talk some sense into her.

"You got it, Dad," she promised. "I can't wait to show you my new Porsche."

New Porsche? He sighed. *It was hard to compete with that.* "Love you, honey."

"Love you too, Dad," she said, then disconnected the line.

She looked at her watch. She'd have plenty of time to wrap everything up before Tucker got home.

CHAPTER 12

It felt like deja vu. A hiker found another dead man at Birchwood Park not more than fifty yards from the site of Garrett Holt's corpse. This time, a fox terrier had wriggled out of its collar when chasing a squirrel. The owner tracked him down and found him sniffing the body. The second murder victim left in Birchwood Park in less than three months. Isaac scratched his head. *Did they have a serial killer on the loose? Was this park becoming the mob's killing ground?*

Needless to say, this new find would evoke panic throughout the community. And due to that panic, the community would be on heightened alert, noticing every little thing that might be a bit unusual or out of the ordinary. While the police force appreciated the public's help, it also meant they would be inundated with calls asking them to check on every unfamiliar person walking in the area, any unusual noise in someone's backyard, and any unknown vehicle in the neighborhood.

Certainly, the police department would do all they could to calm the residents: they'd increase park patrols, they'd place police vehicles about the neighborhood, and they'd promptly answer the 911 calls, but it would take a lot of manpower working long shifts. And worst of all, Petruco would be more than agitated, he'd be stirring everyone up like a Kitchen Aid mixer on high speed.

A light drizzle was all that was left of the thunderstorm of earlier that day. Still, Isaac's umbrella was more or less functionally ineffective as gusts of wind caught the mist that hung in the air and propelled it horizontally. He pulled the collar of his raincoat up around his neck.

"Bullet to the back of the skull. Right through the brain," Cynthia said, looking like a life-sized gumdrop in her bright red raincoat with the hood pulled over her head.

Isaac held his umbrella over her as she leaned over the deceased. It was important to him that she view the body before they moved it to see if she noticed any similarities between the killings.

"Died instantly," she concluded. "Unlike the first victim who most certainly laid there for several hours as his organs shut down."

Tom walked up from behind and cringed at Cynthia's statement. Not only was it unnecessary, it couldn't be easy for Isaac to be reminded of the gruesomeness of that sight and the shock his young daughter was recovering from. It was something Tom knew about first-hand.

"Close range," she continued. "Whoever pulled the trigger had to be splattered with the victim's blood. It's probably splayed over a pretty good area here."

And being washed away by the rain, Isaac thought to himself.

"No discoloration other than lividity," Cynthia said. "This happened early this morning."

"Why is the body twisted like that?" Isaac asked. The victim's head was bent somewhat under his chest and turned to the right, but his left arm stuck out the left side in a contorted, angular position.

Tom bent down to take a closer look. "Looks like something was pulled out from underneath him."

"From the way his knees are bent, it looks like he was kneeling," Isaac added. "So, it seems whatever he was kneeling over, someone else wanted."

Tom nodded. "Agreed."

He probably didn't even see it coming, Isaac thought to himself. A blast of wind took hold of the umbrella pulling it away. "Have you seen enough?" he asked Cynthia.

"Yes. I'll know more after the autopsy," she said.

"Then let's get out of this weather."

When they reached the parking lot, Cynthia put her hand on Tom's forearm. "Detective Bryant, lucky for you, I happen to be free this evening. You and I can discuss my findings over dinner."

She wanted to discuss these two dead bodies over dinner? He could not think of anything more macabre. "Thank you, Cynthia, but I already have plans."

"So, change them."

"No, Cynthia I can't do that." Eager to escape, he opened the passenger side door of Isaac's car.

"I won't take no for an answer."

"Well I'm afraid you'll have to, Cynthia, as I just told you, I can't." He quickly took a seat in the car with his hand ready to pull the door closed.

She pushed the hood off her head and bent down. "My treat. Lynhall at 7:00 p.m.?"

Isaac leaned over from the driver's seat to intervene. "Sorry, Cynthia, Tom's helping me on a time sensitive issue that I can't get into right now."

Tom nodded. "Yes, that's right. Sorry, Cynthia. We can't get into it right now." Tom gave Isaac a friendly slap on the back.

Cynthia looked back and forth between the men. "Well, all right then."

They both smiled at her.

The team came to get the body, distracting Cynthia. She stood and watched. "No, don't pick him up like that, you idiot," she hollered at one of the men. She looked back at Isaac and Tom. "I've got to get over there before those imbeciles screw it all up." She put the hood back over her silky hair. "But, don't worry, Tom, I'll make room for you in my calendar another time." She marched over to the body shouting "Stop! Stop! Stop!"

Isaac looked over at Tom. "I can't keep bailing you out, you know."

"Is this why your former partner moved to California?" Tom asked.

♦♦♦

Tucker pushed his horn-rimmed glasses back up the sharp slope of his nose with his middle finger and then re-straightened the briefcase he had placed on the desk in front of him after returning from his morning meeting hours before. He stood and paced once again in front of the window watching the traffic on Seventh Street below. He had put in a great performance this morning. *An award-winning performance*. But how could it be otherwise? He had the best team in the state supporting him thanks to his father's connections. They made sure he remained on top of everything and anything that went on in the State, from the inner cities to the most rural reaches of Greater Minnesota. They also made sure he could offer a sensible viewpoint on any topic— with a good backdoor out of it, if necessary. He had been schooled, drilled, rehearsed and groomed for this. He was essentially a product. A product that was now being test marketed. He just hoped all those in attendance were sold.

He looked at his watch. Three minutes to five. Why hadn't they contacted him yet? He had expected a call or even a visitor by now. He tapped his pencil on his desk. He moved the stapler to the right. But, these things take time, he supposed. It would be fine. He picked up the phone and dialed.

"Yes, Tucker?" his assistant Shirley, answered.

"Any calls for me?"

"No, still no calls," Shirley answered.

"Okay. I'm taking off."

She looked at the clock on her computer. Five o'clock. "Okay. Have a wonderful weekend up north."

"Thanks."

Tucker put on his suit coat, picked up the briefcase and set off for the elevators, making a point to smile, wave and nod at those he passed on his way. In politics, popularity was everything.

He pulled his Mercedes out of the parking garage and into the traffic on Marquette Avenue, taking his usual route. The air was thick and the sky had the greenish hue that follows a stormy day. He loosened his tie and turned up the air as the windows began to steam up inside the car.

Tucker fell in behind a long line of traffic backed up along Birchwood Parkway and slowly passed by the police vehicles, emergency vehicles and television vans lining the road. His windshield wipers swished back and forth clearing the water that dripped off the trees along the boulevard. He pushed his glasses up and squinted through the window trying to get a look at the scene, but a honk from behind made him move along. He hadn't been notified about this yet, but expected he would be soon.

A few blocks down he pulled into his garage and shut the door. It had been a stressful day, but it was done.

He entered the kitchen and threw his keys in the ceramic dish on the counter. It was time for a little celebration. But not too much. He needed to be ready for an eventful evening. They were sure to contact him soon. He opened the refrigerator and pulled out a beer. He twisted off the cap and took a long pull from the bottle. *Man, that tasted good.*

He entered the living room and stopped dead in his tracks. There she was lying back in the recliner doing some online shopping. "You're here?"

"Surprise," Nikki said.

It certainly was a surprise.

She touched the "buy now" button. "Yeah, Hans cancelled our session today. He's sick."

She wasn't supposed to be here. "Sick?"

She pointed at the beer in his hand. "It must have gone well."

This would certainly change his plans. "What?"

"Your big presentation. Wasn't that today?"

"Yes. Right."

"So, how did it go?"

"Not as I had expected."

"No? Oh, that's too bad."

"Yes," he agreed. "It sure is." He took a gulp of beer.

"Well, Tucker, you can't win 'em all," she said as she laid the laptop on the coffee table.

"Uh huh."

"With all the lies and deceit in politics these days, you never know who you can trust. But I'm sure things are about to change for you."

He pushed the glasses back up his nose with his middle finger. "Right."

"Hey, honey," she said. "Before you get too comfortable, would you mind getting us some take out from Golden Dragon? I've had a craving for some shrimp egg foo young all day."

"Sure." That helped. Now he had the excuse he needed to get away. There were a few things he needed to take care of — privately.

"Perfect." She gave him a thumbs up. "Thanks."

CHAPTER 13

"Another dead man at Birchwood Park?" Peg exclaimed as Isaac entered the station.

Isaac nodded.

"The phone is going to be ringing off the hook."

If anyone wanted to know anything about what was going on at the station, Peg was your contact. New cases, cold cases or personal tidbits about anyone at the precinct, Peg would know. She'd been employed there for as long as Isaac could remember, starting when she was a young girl just out of high school. She befriended everyone and was a busy body of the highest caliber.

"It's going to be crazy!" she added.

Isaac nodded in sympathy. *Oh yes. Two dead bodies found within a week of each other at the same location?* It would keep them both busy. "Tom's on his way in," he told her.

"Tom Bryant?"

"Yes. Would you let him know I'll be in the meeting room down the hall?"

"It would be my pleasure." She grinned. "You sure know how to pick 'em, Isaac."

"Pick them?"

"Partners. Tom's even hotter than Vick." She winked. "I'm looking forward to getting to know him better."

Isaac laughed. "Peg, you little vixen. Aren't you still dating Red?"

"Oh, I most certainly am, but that doesn't mean I've gone blind."

Isaac headed down the hall toward the meeting room, but stopped half way. Peg's comment reminded him what he told Cynthia he and Tom would be doing tonight. He hadn't told a lie. This time sensitive issue certainly needed their attention, but just in case, he'd better make sure. "Peg," he called out. "If Cynthia Chu calls for either Tom or me, please tell her we can't be interrupted."

"You got it."

Isaac sat at the conference table with the evidence laid out in front of him. They didn't have much. A prepaid cell phone, a gas station receipt and a half smoked joint, each in their protective plastic bag. He'd turn it all over to the forensics team, but first he wanted to look the items over while they were still fresh. One of the florescent lights in the ceiling was failing; it flickered and buzzed overhead, momentarily interrupting his focus. He made a mental note to have Peg tell maintenance about it.

He picked up the bag containing the receipt and googled the name of the station, then jotted down the address. That would be his first stop. With so little to go on, at least it would be a start.

No wallet, keys, fobs or identification of any kind was found on the body. The victim's jacket had been thrown up across his back giving the impression that it had been searched. There was a bloody smear across the rear of his jeans indicating that the killer had also removed something from his back pocket. Most likely, his wallet. It also appeared to all at the scene that something large had been pulled out from underneath the victim as well. *Had it been a simple robbery gone bad?* The victim was clean and reasonably groomed, so he didn't look like a homeless vagrant. Needless to say, they would certainly keep an eye on any reported missing persons. If this man had family, a call would come in soon.

It was evident that the victim had been lying there since prior to the rainstorm of the early morning because the ground beneath the body was dry. That would mean the murder happened before 4:40 a.m., and that was not a good sign. Who was out at 4:40 a.m. in the woods of Birchwood Park? Only those up to no good.

Much of the victim's face was missing or had been shattered by the bullet, so it would be very hard to identify him using mug shots. His fingerprints had been taken and his blood drawn, so they were looking for a match. But, for these identifiers to be in the system, he'd have to have been a criminal. More specifically, a criminal who had been arrested.

The most curious thing, was that the pre-paid cell phone was found inside the victim's sock. They discovered it when they went to lift the body onto the gurney. Why? He had plenty of pockets in his clothing. For Isaac, it was just another indicator that this wasn't someone out for an early morning walk who happened to run into trouble.

So, what did these two victims have in common? From what Isaac currently knew, it seemed easier to make a list of the things they didn't have in common. He could only hope the forensics results would give them the answers— or at least a lead.

As if in answer to his thoughts, Tom came through the door with a handful of photos.

"Jefe," he said. "Look at these." He dropped the photos on the table.

An hour earlier the owner of a restaurant down the road from Birchwood Park had called. He had found some unusual, excess garbage in his dumpster. This had become a regular occurrence for the business owner. People who didn't want to pay to rid themselves of items that were not allowed in their regular trash cans, would thoughtlessly chuck them in his. He'd seen all kinds of refuse from paint cans to metal swing sets, and it all took up space in the receptacle he paid for, leaving no room for his own garbage. So, every time he found some offending waste, he'd report it to the police. This time he'd found a large duffle bag.

Isaac spread the photos on the table. "What's the story?"

"The restaurant owner went to dump his trash like he does every day, and found this duffle bag." Tom leaned over and tapped the appropriate photo with his pointer finger. "He called the cops to report the intrusion— just like he always does." He pulled out a chair, twirled it around and straddled it. "And just like they always do, the cops in the area showed up. But this time, they noticed this wasn't just some old unrecyclable junk someone tried to get rid of. They saw blood on the bag." He let his words hang in the air for a moment to get the full impact.

"So, the officers called it in." Isaac said.

"Exactly. So, forensics came and bagged the duffle and took it to the lab for testing." He tapped on a few photos on the right. "These are some pictures of what was inside."

Isaac perused the photos. "Hunting clothes?"

"Yep."

The blood splatter was considerable. "They're covered. The person wearing these was very close to their victim."

"Yep."

"I'm assuming we're running tests now to see if it matches the victim's blood type?"

"Yep."

A good development, yes, but a bit of a scary development. *Hunting clothes in April? Hunting clothes in Birchwood Park?* Only a large animal would produce this much blood splatter and Isaac knew that deer hunting season was in the fall. If these were the clothes worn by the victim's killer, it looked less and less like a robbery or drug deal gone wrong.

It was a silly question, but Isaac had to ask. "Any identification labels on the clothing or duffle?"

"None we saw on first examination. High quality stuff, though."

"You said they found blood on the outside of the duffle?"

"Oh yes, Jefe. Lots of it." Tom raised his brows. "I think the duffle is what was pulled out from underneath the dead guy's body."

"So, it would seem that the killer wanted whatever was inside."

"It would seem," Tom agreed. "And even more intriguing . . ." He tapped on another photo. "There was newspaper at the bottom of the bag." The newspaper had been cut into strips and laid along the bottom of the bag.

Did the something inside need padding? "Was there any impression left on the newspaper?"

"Not to the naked eye. But I'm sure forensics will check."

Isaac sat back in his chair and folded his arms across his chest. "They didn't happen to find a gun there too, did they?"

Tom let out a laugh. "Nope. Sorry, Jefe."

"Did the restaurant owner have security cameras?"

"He did, right over the dumpster as a matter of fact."

Isaac looked at Tom hopefully.

"But he said vandals knocked it down just a week ago." Tom pointed out the photo of the camera that hung useless from its holder now taking footage of the brick wall. "He said no one was available to fix it until next week."

"Let's check the neighboring businesses." They could always hope that footage would surface showing an identifiable person carrying that duffle bag. After all, it had to get there somehow.

They heard a knock at the door and Joyce stepped in. "Isaac I've come to get the evidence." She set a plastic bin on the table, then turned her attention to Tom. "I don't believe we've met. I'm Joyce. From forensics." Her eyes twinkled and she held out her hand to him.

Tom stood and gave it a gentle shake. "Tom," he said. "Isaac's new partner."

Isaac watched the exchange looking for a glimmer of interest on Tom's part. *Maybe this could be a good match?* "Nice to see you, Joyce," Isaac said. "Are you still helping out at Friends of the Orphans?"

"Oh yes, those kids are just great." She cocked her head at Tom. "Do you like kids, Tom?"

"I do," Tom said. "In fact, I used to be one myself."

They all laughed.

"Tom's from Wisconsin," Isaac added.

"Oh?" Joyce said. "My grandmother was from Door County, we visited every summer."

"How nice," Tom responded."

There was an uncomfortable silence.

"Well, it's nice to meet you Tom. I look forward to getting to know you."

"Thank you," Tom replied. "It's nice to meet you too."

"The pleasure is all mine," Joyce said, hoping to encourage an invitation for coffee or something, but Tom said no more.

"Well," Isaac interjected, realizing this was going nowhere, "Enough with the pleasantries. Let's get back to business." He started to deposit the evidence in the bin, when suddenly, the cell phone that had been pulled from the victim's sock began ringing. Isaac quickly picked up a pen and wrote the caller's number on his notepad. The caller ID said "Tuck Rennicke." *Why did that name sound familiar?*

Isaac answered through the plastic bag. "Tuck?" he asked.

"What the hell happened?" screamed the voice on the other end.

"What happened?" Isaac asked.

There was a long pause. "Wait, who is this? Where's Richie?"

"Richie? Is this Richie's phone?" Isaac asked.

"Stop messing with me, damn it. Who is this?"

"This is Detective Isaac Scott of the Minneapolis Police Department. Who is this?"

Silence. "Yeah, right. Sure it is," the caller said and hung up.

CHAPTER 14

Isaac maneuvered through the gas station lot, careful not to drive his vehicle into any of the large craters dotting the asphalt, and found a spot on the side of the small building. He stepped out of the car and onto the sidewalk. The spring rain had rejuvenated the weeds that grew abundantly between the cracks in the concrete.

A cloud of smoke greeted him as he rounded the corner. "Hello," he said to the woman standing there as she took another drag of her cigarette.

She inhaled and flipped a hand at him in response.

It was a small enough establishment, so hopefully, that meant someone would recognize the victim. He entered the store and walked over to the man in the Grateful Dead T-shirt behind the counter.

"What can I do for you?" the man asked.

Isaac introduced himself and asked if the owner or manager was available.

"You're looking at him."

Isaac held out the receipt. "I'm trying to identify the man who made this purchase."

The man examined the receipt. "It's ours," he confirmed.

"May I look at your security videos for that day and time?"

"Anything to help the cops," the man replied. "I'd like to see more of you in this neighborhood." He came out from behind the counter. "Just a second," he said to Isaac. He opened the door and hollered at the woman. "Dahlia, get in here."

Through the dirty window, Isaac watched her snub out her cigarette and trudge inside.

"Yeah?" she said, obviously unhappy to have been interrupted.

"Watch the store. I'm going in the back."

Dahlia scrutinized Isaac. "What's up?"

"Just watch the store," he responded, then turned to Isaac. "I'm Dean, by the way." He reached out a hand.

Isaac shook it.

"What was the date and time again?" Dean asked as he opened the door to his office.

"Thursday evening at 8:37 p.m."

Dean's office looked more like a large closet than an office as it was stashed with boxes of windshield washer fluid, engine oil and cartons of cigarettes. He spun the tattered office chair around and sat down.

"So, what did he do?"

"Not sure if he did anything. I'm just trying to identify him."

Dean powered up his computer and found the security footage for the date and time. Isaac leaned over his shoulder.

They watched as a man exited a truck and walked up to the store. He was about the same size and build of the victim, but since much of the victim's face was missing, it would be difficult to confirm a positive identification without corroborating evidence.

"That's Richie," Dean said. "But I've never seen that truck before. He usually drives a beat-up Chevy Cavalier, kind of a silver color."

Bingo. "Do you know Richie's last name?"

"Nah. He always pays in cash. Wonder where this one came from? Looks almost new," Dean continued, still focused on the truck. "Do you think he stole it?"

Isaac ignored the question. "What can you tell me about Richie?"

"Nice enough, but I always kept an eye on him when he was in the store. He had some sticky fingers, if you know what I mean. Played the pull tabs. Won enough to keep him coming back for more." He sized-up Isaac. He didn't look like a narc, but you never know. From what Dean had seen, drugs would be the end of this neighborhood. "Always smelled like weed," he added.

"Do you know if he had a job?"

"Not that I know of, but he seemed to have some money to spend lately. Used to be he'd be counting the pennies out at my counter. I let him take some stuff even if he didn't have quite enough." He shrugged. "You know, trying to help him out."

"Did he mention any family?"

"Nah, I think he came from a small town up north somewhere."

"Any idea where he lives?"

"Oh sure." He pointed to the apartment building across the street. "He lives there."

Why didn't I ask that to begin with? Isaac thought to himself. "Can you print me a picture from the video?"

♦♦♦

Isaac took the photocopy and crossed the street. He entered the vestibule of the apartment building and scanned the names of the residents on the mailboxes. They were all labeled with a first initial and last name. Fortunately, it was a small building and only four residents had the first initial of "R." He decided to start on the first floor and work his way up to the third, if necessary. First stop, apartment number 9 belonging to R. Quiddler. He walked up the half flight of stairs and down the dark, dank hallway. He arrived at the second apartment with the number 6 on the door and figured he must be in the right place since he had already passed apartments one through eight. He gave the number a little tap with his pointer finger and it swung back and forth. He knocked.

No answer.

He put his ear to the door. All was quiet.

He turned, took a small step across the narrow hallway and knocked on the door of apartment number 10.

A dark shadow covered the eyehole. "Who is it?" a woman's voice asked from inside.

"Detective Isaac Scott of the Minneapolis Police Department," Isaac responded, then held up his badge for her review.

He heard the chain slide from the slot and the lock turn. The door opened wide. "How can I help?" asked the round-faced matron wearing an oven mitt.

Isaac held up the picture. "Do you know this man?"

"I do. That's Richie. He lives across the hall."

Amazing. First try. "May I ask you some questions about Richie?"

"You betcha. Is he in trouble? Has he been arrested?"

How was he to answer those questions? "He has not been arrested. He might be in trouble." *Or dead*, Isaac thought to himself.

"Come in. I just made some cookies."

Isaac stepped through the door. The room took him back in time to the 1960s. She led him past the harvest gold Naugahyde sofa on tapered wooden stick legs, that sat across from the large television set still sporting an antenna, into the kitchen and directed him to sit at the silver metal table with the gray swirled Formica top. She opened the oven door and the aroma of sugar cookies filled the room. She set the cookie sheet on the stove top. "Just wait a minute while I get these others in."

Isaac watched the tail that hung from the black and white cat wall clock swing back and forth counting the seconds.

"Take a seat," she instructed.

Isaac pulled out a chair that reminded him of the ones his grandmother had when he was a child, right down to the crackling in the padded plastic cushion.

She set the second cookie sheet on the middle rack of the oven and closed the door. "He's a good boy, but always seemed to be looking for trouble," she said. She pulled off the oven mitt and set it on the counter. "Just got mixed up with the wrong crowd. Men are banging on his door almost weekly. I think Richie owes a lot of people money. I try to look after him as best I can. I always open my door and threaten to call the police when I hear the yelling to get rid of the riff raff. Usually it works." She turned the dial on the timer that looked like a white chicken sitting on its nest. "Just last Wednesday, a man actually threatened to kill Richie. It was frightening." She set the timer on the table and sat down across from Isaac. "The worst part is, I think it was his father."

"Threatened to kill him?"

She nodded vigorously. "Yes, I heard it loud and clear."

"What exactly did you hear?"

"He said, 'I'm gonna kill you.'"

"And you think this was Richie's father?"

Her eyes widened. "Yes."

"Had you seen this man before?"

"No. But he called Richie 'son' and said Richie stole his truck."

That would answer where Richie got the truck Dean didn't recognize. "How did you hear this?"

"Because he was yelling. The whole building probably heard him. I asked him to quiet down, but he kept yelling. He was quite worked up."

"Did you get a good look at him?"

She nodded.

"Could you identify him?"

"Absolutely."

Maybe he was getting somewhere. "When did you last see Richie?"

"Yesterday."

"Yesterday?" Isaac furrowed his brow. "What time?"

"Oh, it was very early in the morning."

If this Richie was one and the same as the victim they found yesterday, it certainly would have to have been. *Was it possible he worked an early shift?* "Is that usual for him to be up early?"

"No. That wasn't usual for him. He stays out pretty late some nights, but yesterday he didn't come home until just after the sun came up."

"You said he *came home* early yesterday morning? You didn't see him *leave* early yesterday morning?"

"That's right. Whenever I hear a noise in the hallway, I look out the eyehole on the door. You have to be careful in this neighborhood. Things have changed a lot since I moved in forty years ago. I take it upon myself to check in with our little family here." She smiled at Isaac. "That's what the cookies are for. I'm visiting the third floor today. No one can say no to a plate of cookies."

Came home yesterday after the sun was up? That didn't make sense. Could he have the wrong man? "Are you sure it was Richie?"

"Yes, I think so. He was wearing that sweatshirt with the bald eagle on the back he always wears."

"Did you see his face?"

She paused and thought about it for a moment. "No, he was putting the key in the door."

"Was the hood up?"

She nodded slowly. "Yes, I believe it was."

CHAPTER 15

Red rolled out of bed and didn't bother to shower. He stepped into the torn jeans that were two sizes too big and cinched the belt just enough so they hung low, but wouldn't fall off. He pulled on the gray T-shirt that hadn't been washed for over two weeks and slid into his old sneakers.

Peg was up at the kitchen table sipping coffee. They'd only been dating for two months, but she was already secretly shopping for wedding rings. She had no intention of letting a good man like Red get away. On first meeting Red, most would describe him as easy going and complacent — practically to the point of being apathetic. But Peg knew that underneath that benign exterior, was a man full of daring and courage; a man who cared very deeply and actually craved a little danger in his life. She loved that about him. "Good morning, sleepy head," she said with that little squeak in her voice he found so endearing.

He smiled at the sound. "Good morning, my love." Red had been smitten with Peg since the day they met at the station. Red wasn't one to shy away from dangerous situations, but it took him over two years to get up the courage to ask her out. Peg was dependable, down to earth, and didn't take herself too seriously. All traits Red found very appealing. But the thing that sent his heart racing, was that when she smiled, he could see the little gap between her two front teeth. She was the kind of woman a man could settle down with, and never once regret it.

She set down her coffee cup. "Looks like another day undercover."

"You know it." He leaned down and kissed the top of her head. "I'm on a mission," he said and he meant it. He'd find Garrett Holt's killer if it killed him. He'd go as deep as he could in the organizational matrix of the mob until he got the answer.

She knew this was his job, and it was one of the things she found so intriguing about him, but it still worried her every time he walked out the door. "When am I going to be able to wash those stinky clothes?"

He held up crossed fingers. "Getting closer every day."

He went outside and dug in the garden making sure to get the dirt under his fingernails. He tied the bandana around his head, tufts of his curly red hair puffed out on the top and bottom, and walked with purpose to the bus stop. It was a beautiful day, but all he could think of was exonerating himself for losing Garrett Holt last February. He'd hit dead ends so far, but with each day came new hope.

♦♦♦

Once downtown, Red set out to find Hugo. Hugo was a delivery boy for the bookies who always had his ears wide open. If anybody could give him more details about what was happening in gangland, it would be Hugo.

Red found him on the street corner on Fourth and Hennepin, pan handling; something he really didn't need to do. Hugo made good money and owned a nice home in northeast Minneapolis. It was more likely he was put on that street corner to be a look out or to watch for something in particular. Then he'd send a message to his employers to alert them.

"Dude," Red said to him, as he shuffled up and shoved his hands in his pockets looking like someone with nowhere in particular to be.

"What's happening, Red?" Hugo asked.

Even on the streets, they called him Red. Most in the criminal community had decided Red was a lazy, harmless druggie of no importance, which was the secret to his success. He was lanky and freckled, and had a casual, lackadaisical way about him that set people at ease.

"What's with all the cops?" Red asked. "They're like everywhere."

Hugo's eyes scanned the street. "They're snooping around trying to find out who killed Garrett Holt."

"Who?"

"Garrett Holt," Hugo repeated.

Red stared blankly at him. It was a look that had been practiced and perfected. Over his years working undercover, he had found that people were more likely to open up if you played ignorant.

"Dude was a big gambler and in for over a hundred grand."

"Shit. Over a hundred grand?" Red shook his head. "Well, if you don't pay the bills, you're gonna get killed."

"Nah, that wasn't it." Hugo watched a white Cadillac make a turn onto Third Street. He opened up his text messages and pressed send.

Red made a mental note of the license plate. "It wasn't the money?"

"Nah." Hugo crammed his cell phone back in his pocket. "He had a rich wife and always came up with the money eventually."

Red put on his best look of total confusion.

Hugo put a hand on Red's shoulder. "So, here's the deal. Holt's wife is killed, leaving him all her millions, see?

So one of the enforcers was supposed to meet with him to encourage him to pay up, but that's the last anybody saw of Holt. Everybody just figured he'd skipped town with his dead wife's money and they've had their connections all over the country trying to track him down. But then, just last week, he turns up dead right here in Birchwood Park."

Red knew what an enforcer could do to encourage, but it sounded like this one went a little too far. "No shit. That's savage. So they're out their money?"

"Hell no. Whoever saw Holt alive last will have to pay up." He raised his eyebrows. "One way or another. They are steaming salty," he said. "Dude was a huge source of income, so whoever killed that cash cow is in deep shit."

Red had already heard this buzz from numerous sources, but he had to play it through to get to the big question. "So the cops and the bookies are looking for the same guy?"

A red Toyota passed by in front of them. "Hold on," Hugo said. He took out his cell phone and sent a one-digit text.

Red added the license plate number to his mental list.

"Yeah, same guy." He smiled. "And I got money down on who'll find him first."

Here it was. Red threw up a prayer. "So, who are they looking for?"

Hugo shook his head. "Don't know. Just glad it's not me."

Another dead end on identifying Garrett's killer. Red kicked at a crack in the pavement. "Yeah, straight up," he said.

But maybe all was not lost and Hugo could help connect the dots between Garrett and this new body they found. Red put on his confused face again. "Wasn't there a second dead guy found in Birchwood Park too?"

"Yeah, I heard about that."

"Shit, man. Is that the new dumping ground?"

"Ha! Seriously, dude."

"Have you heard who it was?"

"Some two-bit dealer. Richie somebody."

A name was good. At least he'd have something to report. "Was he in deep too?"

He shrugged. "Small time, man. Not worth it."

CHAPTER 16

Isaac pulled in next to the curb in front of the stately two-story Tudor. He knew that a person had to be doing pretty well financially to afford to live in this neighborhood. It was the sort of neighborhood others of lessor means drove through just to admire the large homes, manicured lawns and well-tended gardens.

Isaac noticed lights on inside the house that had not been on his last two visits. That was a good sign. Now he hoped Tucker was home. And not only home, but willing to talk with him. However, since Tucker had not responded to any of his telephone calls or returned any of his messages, he had his doubts.

The smaller of the three garage doors opened and a young woman with white blond hair and bright pink spandex pushed a yellow bicycle out to the driveway. Isaac quickly removed himself from the car. "Good morning," he called to her. "I'm Detective Isaac Scott with the Minneapolis Police Department and I'm looking for a man named Tucker." He held out his badge. "I believe he lives here?"

A Cadillac backed out from the house next door and stopped in the driveway.

"Yeah, Tucker lives here," the woman said. She waved to her neighbor. "Good morning, Frank," she called.

Isaac started up the driveway.

The elderly neighbor lowered his car window and eyed Isaac nervously. "Everything okay, Nikki?"

"Everything's fine, Frank."

Frank stared at Isaac for a moment longer and then continued out of the driveway. He decided to go around the block and check back just to be sure.

Isaac tried not to take offense. They probably didn't see many Black men in this high-end neighborhood and with the recent discovery of two dead men in the nearby park, people had a reason to be cautious. Certainly, everyone was on edge, but still, he knew that look and had to wonder if things would ever change.

"Sorry," the young woman said to Isaac. "Frank's a privileged shithead."

Isaac laughed at her comment.

She leaned her bike against the garage wall. "Tuck's inside. I'm his wife, Nikki. Let me show you in."

Nikki led him between the Mercedes sedan and the Porsche convertible into the expansive kitchen. Rich cherry kitchen cabinets lined the walls interspersed with top-of-the-line stainless steel appliances sporting all the latest features. There was counterspace galore and a large screen television hung above the scroll top desk. It was a kitchen Isaac's gourmet wife would die for.

"Tucker," Nikki called out loudly. "There's someone here to see you."

Tucker came into the kitchen dressed in a suit and tie. "What?" he asked impatiently.

She gestured toward Isaac. "There's someone here to see you," she repeated.

Isaac reached out his hand. "I'm Detective Isaac Scott with the Minneapolis Police Department. I believe we spoke on the telephone last Friday."

Tucker blinked. "That was for real?"

"Yes," Isaac said.

Tucker took Isaac's hand and shook it. "I thought one of Richie's friends stole his phone." He pushed his horn-rimmed glasses back up his nose with his middle finger. "You must forgive me, Detective. I had no idea. Richie had some nefarious friends." He looked to his wife. "Isn't that right, Nikki?"

She crinkled her brow. "Richie Quiddler?"

Tucker nodded.

"Yeah, I guess so." She looked back and forth between the two of them. *They had a conversation on Richie's phone? How did that happen?*

"Quiddler was Richie's last name?" Isaac asked. Just further confirmation he had been at the right apartment building.

They both nodded.

"Q-u-i-d-d-l-e-r," Nikki said. "What's this about?"

"Perhaps we should all sit down," Isaac suggested. "And I can fill you in."

"Okay," Tucker said. "But I don't have much time. I have a very important meeting in an hour that I need to prepare for."

"This won't take long," Isaac said. Actually, he had no idea how long it would take, but he needed to take advantage of having Tucker in front of him. After his calls and messages went unanswered for two days, he didn't believe he'd get another opportunity any time soon. "I called several times, but did not get an answer, so I thought it best to come here personally."

"You called?" Tucker readjusted his glasses with his index finger and thumb. "I'm sorry, my election committee takes care of all my calls and messages." He pulled out a stool and took a seat at the large, granite covered, center island that took up the middle of the room. "I don't know if you know, but I'm running for state representative. And, since throwing my hat into the ring, I am constantly inundated with calls from the press, special interest groups and the like. It would be impossible for me to address them all, so the committee takes care of all of that for me," he said in explanation. "We just got back from a weekend up north, so I can check into it, but I imagine one of them will be returning your calls shortly."

"I understand," Isaac replied. Did he? You'd think a call from a police detective would get a reasonably quick response, but on the other hand, his messages had only requested a return call, so in fairness, he supposed they could have thought he was fundraising for the department.

"Please, Detective, take a seat." Nikki said and chose the stool next to her husband. "Now, what's this about Richie?"

Isaac sat across from them. He pulled out the photocopy from the gas station security footage and laid it on the counter in front of them. "Is this Richie?"

They both nodded.

"You both knew Richie?"

Nikki pulled the photo closer. She had the fingernails of someone who never lifted a finger. "Richie and I went to high school together," Nikki said. "Actually, we were in school together from grade school on up."

In reality, she probably knew Richie better than anyone. Richie Quiddler who always pushed the limits. Who was always getting into things he shouldn't have been getting into. Who never respected the rules. She'd never forget that evening back in sixth grade when they walked home together from Tuesday night bingo at the town hall and she got her first taste of what Richie was capable of.

♦♦♦

The wind had whipped up white caps on the water as they crossed the bridge over Lake Roosevelt. Nikki had held on to her long braids to keep them from blowing around like ropes in the breeze. The town had closed down for the night and the only light visible on Main Street was the neon 7 Up sign in the grocery store window. It called to her.

"I'm thirsty," she said.

"You are?" Richie smiled mischievously. "Leave it up to me." He picked up a large rock from the side of the road and ran up the sidewalk to the front door of the store.

"What are you doing?" Nikki called after him.

"You're thirsty." He gave her a wink and smashed the glass.

The store didn't have a security system. There hadn't been a need for that kind of thing in Plummer's Point until Richie Quiddler came along.

"Stay away from that kid," her dad had warned. "He's no good."

From that time on, Richie got blamed for any mishap in town. From the scratch on Mr. Ballard's car to Mrs. Lawson's missing cat. Tucker may have called him nefarious, but Nikki knew better. He was just bored.

♦♦♦

Tucker pushed the photo back toward Isaac. "My family has a cabin in Nikki's hometown and that's how I got to know Richie," Tucker explained. "His dad owns a gas station and auto repair shop there."

"So," Isaac said. "When we spoke and you thought I was Richie, you asked me what happened. What was that about?" *Asked* wasn't exactly the correct word to use to describe how that question had been posed, but he didn't need to stir things up just now.

Tucker shifted in his seat. "Richie was supposed to meet me and he never showed." He widened his bulging eyes and did a quick jiggle of his head in what appeared to be frustration. "He was very unpredictable, so I must apologize for my tone that evening."

"You were supposed to meet with Richie?" Nikki asked Tucker.

"Yes," he admitted. "I wanted to tell you, but Richie made me promise to keep it a secret." He readjusted his glasses with his index finger and thumb. "I was giving him money to help him get out of his situation. You know how proud he could be."

Proud wouldn't have been one of the characteristics Nikki would've used to describe Richie, but she kept that to herself. "You were giving him money?"

Tucker nodded, then turned toward Isaac. "Richie was involved with some bad people. Gambling. Drugs. He needed money to pay everyone off and then was going to leave town and start anew. He seemed sincere, but he kept missing appointments and then, at the same time, was asking for more money. Understandably, I was getting a little frustrated."

"You were giving Richie Quiddler money?" Nikki repeated. "How in the world did you think that was a good idea?"

"I was helping him out." He gave her a dirty look.

She returned it. "How much? How much did you give him?"

"Let's not waste the detective's time, dear. We can discuss this later." He gave her a forced smile and patted her leg.

She shoved his hand away, but kept quiet.

Tucker set his elbows on the countertop, dying to ask the burning question. "Detective," he said. "How did you happen to have Richie's phone?"

Isaac didn't need to get into any details. In fact, at this point of the investigation, the less detail given to any interviewee the better. While from all accounts Richie was involved in some dangerous activities, they had not clearly identified any suspect or motivation for the murder. "Richie is dead," he said simply.

"What?" they said in unison.

"His body was found last Friday. He had the phone with him."

"Oh my God," Tucker said.

Isaac let the news sink in and watched them. Nikki covered her face with her hands. Tucker looked crestfallen, betrayed and angry all at once.

"What happened to him?" Tucker asked.

"That's what we're trying to find out," Isaac answered. "Do you know how we can get in touch with his next of kin?"

Nikki lowered her hands. "I do," she said. "His mother will be devastated."

That provided the perfect segue for Isaac's next questions. "What kind of relationship did Richie have with his parents?"

"He was very close to his mother," Nikki said. "She stood up for him whenever he got into trouble—which was a lot. His dad, Glen, was another story. Their relationship was strained at best." She leaned in as people do when they're about to share some gossip. "See, rumor has it that Richie was the product of his mother's affair with one of the citiots."

Tucker gave her another dirty look.

"I mean 'seasonal visitors'," she said correcting herself.

"Citiots?" Isaac asked.

"Yeah, it's a combination of the words 'city' and 'idiot'." She shrugged. "That's what the northerners call people from the cities."

"Clever."

"Yeah, there are a few smart people in the country."

Tucker gave her another dirty look.

How did these two ever get together? Isaac wondered.

"Anyway," Nikki continued. "Glen put up with Richie for his wife's sake, but he was never completely able to accept him. Richie was a constant reminder of his wife's infidelity. Glen and Richie fought about everything, and poor Caroline was stuck in the middle."

"Caroline is Richie's mother's name?" Isaac asked.

"Yes, that's right. It was a pretty sorry state of affairs. And for some unknown reason, Richie liked nothing better than to push Glen to the limit."

"I heard him threaten to kill Richie more than once," Tucker volunteered.

Nikki sat back. She hadn't considered that. "Oh, that was all just talk," she said dismissing his comment. "Glen would never do that."

It was at this point that Tucker insisted he had to go.

"Just one final question, if you please," Isaac said. "Do either of you know Garrett Holt?"

Tucker stood and straightened his suitcoat. "Wasn't he the one found murdered in Birchwood Park last week?"

"Yes."

"No," they both said in unison.

Tucker adjusted his tie. "Do you think these murders are related?"

Did he? They were both gamblers found dead in the same park. "We are just beginning to collect the facts, Mr. Rennicke," Isaac responded. "So we haven't drawn any conclusions, but are looking at all possibilities."

Tucker pushed the glasses up his nose. "It sounds like a gang war."

Isaac certainly hoped not. "I appreciate your time." He placed his business card on the countertop. "If you think of anything you'd like to add, please call me."

Nikki gave Isaac the contact information for Richie's parents. "Please call Glen about this. Then he can give the news to Caroline."

They all left the residence together. Tucker got in the Mercedes and Nikki straddled her bike.

As Isaac walked down the driveway to his car, a black and white pulled up in front of it. The officer got out of the car. "Isaac!"

"Muhammed. Good to see you. What brings you to this neighborhood?"

"We had a report of a suspicious man lingering at this address."

Isaac looked over at his shoulder toward the neighbor's house and sighed. "That would be me."

CHAPTER 17

Isaac returned to the station and took a moment to jot down some notes to record the morning's events. It seemed rather irrational to Isaac that Tucker Rennicke had given Richie money to buy Richie out of his trouble. And Tucker's wife made it clear she felt the same, which made him wonder if there was more to that story. That explanation just didn't hold water, and the underlying tension between the couple was palpable. Whether that held any weight or not, was hard to decipher. However, since they had just started on the investigation, he thought it best not to press too hard at this time. But after the investigators had collected more facts about the murder, he'd be back with some more pointed questions.

Isaac picked up his phone and, as Nikki had requested, dialed the number for Glen Quiddler's gas station in Plummer's Point.

The phone was answered on the fifth ring. "Glen's Gas and Garage, this is Adam."

There was so much background noise, Isaac had to plug his right ear with his middle finger so he could concentrate on what was coming through the phone in his left ear. "May I speak to Glen Quiddler, please?"

"Hey Rod, can you stop that for a second? I'm on the phone," Adam yelled. "Sorry about that," he said to Isaac. "Glen's not here."

"Do you know when he'll be back?"

"Probably tomorrow."

Isaac heard the squeal of a garage door opening. "Is there a way to reach him before then?"

"Hang on a minute," Adam said to Isaac. 'No Rod, back that one up. It's the other one that needs the oil change,' Isaac heard him say. "Glen's picking up a tranny in Minneapolis," Adam told Isaac. "You could try his cell."

He's in Minneapolis? Isaac quickly pulled out a pen and pad of paper. "Good. What's his cell number?"

Adam shouted the number out to Isaac over the revving of an engine.

"Can you tell me where he's staying?"

"With his mom in Edina," Adam said.

There was a loud clanging as if something heavy had just been dropped from a substantial height.

"Can I get an address?" Isaac asked.

"Look, I gotta go," Adam said hastily. "I'll text it to you."

"Great. Thanks."

The line went dead.

Isaac set the phone on his desk. Interesting. Not only had Glen Quiddler been in town earlier in the week, as reported by Mrs. Kilbernie, but it appeared he was still in town. It would be hard to believe he traveled back to Plummer's Point, then returned to Minneapolis between then and now. This put him in the area, with an opportunity to commit the crime. So now, in addition to the bookies and drug dealers, Isaac had two more to add to his list of people who might want Richie Quiddler dead: Tucker Rennicke and Glen Quiddler.

Isaac picked up the phone to fill Tom in on the day's events, but before he could place the call, it started ringing. The caller ID said, 'Tom Bryant.'

"Well, speak of the devil," Isaac said.

"Jefe, they found a gun at the park."

Things were looking up. "Where?"

"In the woods somewhere. I'm going over to check it out."

The gun that killed Garrett or the gun that killed Richie? Or, could he dare to hope that it was the gun that killed both? "Can they tell how long it's been there?"

"They didn't say."

"Okay. Well, I was just about to call you to let you know I may have located one of our suspects."

"No kidding. Who?"

"The victim's father. Remember Richie's neighbor said she heard a man she believed was Richie's father threaten to kill him just a few days ago?"

"Yep."

"Well, I just found out that Richie's father is still in town and staying with his mother in Edina," Isaac said. "Additionally, Tucker Rennicke said he has also heard Richie's dad threaten to kill him. Rather coincidental don't you think?"

"Most definitely. Good work, Jefe."

"I'm going to see Richie's father now. You get over to Birchwood and check out the gun. Then we can meet up and share notes."

"Sounds good."

"Hey, Tom. Take lots of pictures for me."

"Will do, Jefe."

Isaac ended the call just as another one came in. This time it was Claudia.

"Hi honey," Isaac answered.

"You'll never guess who just came to visit me," she said.

This day was just full of riddles. "Who?" he asked.

"Ruth and Rebecca Rupp."

"Who?"

"Edna's daughters."

He knew Edna had two daughters, but he'd never met them. If he recalled correctly, one lived in Florida and the other in Iowa. "Really? Why?"

"They said they are very concerned about their mother," Claudia said, then added derisively, "Now that she has loads of money."

He could almost hear her eyes roll. "Oh."

"Yes, they told me they think their mother should stop working now. They said she's getting too old for the kind of work she does for us."

"I see," Isaac responded. Claudia was not a woman who could be coerced, and he knew this interloping would not sit well with her. "And what did you tell them?"

"I said if they felt that way, they should bring it up with Edna."

"Good answer." He waited for the rest that was sure to come.

"I also told them I'd come to know their mother quite well, and knew Edna would do what Edna wanted to do."

So true, and probably the very reason they decided to try to manipulate others to get the result they desired. "Absolutely."

"I said any decision like that was up to her – and, I added that she's welcome to work for us as long as she wants."

"Yes. Of course."

"They were not happy."

"Boy, that's too bad."

"They don't want us to take advantage of her good nature."

Edna certainly had a good nature, but that didn't mean she wasn't capable of making her own decisions. "Really. Is that what we're doing?" he asked, knowing exactly what the answer would be.

"We most certainly are not!"

He could practically hear the steam rising off the top of her head. "Were they actually asking us to fire Edna?"

"Not in so many words, but yes, I believe they were."

"They must think Edna won't leave unless we *can* her." It warmed his heart thinking that was most likely true.

"My thoughts exactly. And, get this," she added. "Both of them suddenly want her to live with them."

"Imagine that."

CHAPTER 18

Isaac stopped the car in front of the house on Mackey Avenue.

Two people were on the front lawn in the shade of a large maple tree. A heavy-set man who looked to be in his fifties sat in a lawn chair, staring at his cell phone. An elderly woman rested quietly next to him in a wheel chair with a colorful quilt across her lap. A bird feeder hung from the maple tree and a number of nuthatches flitted about, taking turns grabbing a seed, then flying up into the branches to eat it. It was a rather peaceful scene and both parties looked like they were enjoying the beautiful spring day while watching the activities of the quiet neighborhood.

Isaac stepped out of his car and walked toward the house.

The slam of the car door must have alerted the old woman to his presence and her head jerked up. "You get off my property!" she yelled.

The man looked up from his phone. He stood. "Can I help you?" he said in a rather unhelpful voice.

Isaac stayed on the sidewalk. "Are you Glen Quiddler?"

"That depends." He put a hand to his forehead to block the glare of the sun. "Who's asking?"

"I'm Detective Isaac Scott of the Minneapolis Police Department." He pulled out his badge and held it in the air.

The man came over and took a good look at it. Then at Isaac's face.

He looked worried. "Mr. Quiddler?" Isaac asked.

"Yes, I'm Glen Quiddler."

"May I speak with you about your son, Richie?"

Glen put a hand on top of his bald head. "Okay." He looked up and down the neighborhood. "But not out here."

"Right. Perhaps we should sit down inside?"

Glen nodded, then turned back toward the woman. "Okay, Mama. Let's go in for a little while."

She shook her frail fist at Isaac. "Get that man off my property!"

Glen unlocked the wheels and began to push the wheelchair up the ramp. "Don't get all worked up, Mama."

"I don't want him here," she complained.

Glen hit the button that automatically opened the front door. "I don't want him here either," he mumbled as he pushed her through.

"Idella, Mama's coming inside. Can you take over for me for a bit?" Glen asked.

Glen returned to the front door and waved at Isaac to join him.

Isaac walked up the ramp and through the door that was covered with crackled paint. Dark wallpaper covered the hallway walls.

"You'll have to excuse her," Glen said. "She has dementia. Makes her crabbier than ever."

He led the way to a small study off the entry. The shelves were littered with books covered in dust. They looked like they hadn't been opened in decades.

"Not here! Not here!" Mama's shrill voice screamed from somewhere down the hall.

Glen shook his head. "She's just never happy with anything anymore." He gestured for Isaac to sit down. Glen sat behind the desk. His belly stuck out the bottom of his shirt and rested on his lap. "So, what about Richie?"

This was always difficult. Isaac had plausible reason to believe Mr. Quiddler may already know this, but if not, he would be delivering what could be devastating news. He found the best practice in this situation was to be direct.

"Mr. Quiddler, we found a body in Birchwood Park last Friday and we believe it may be Richie."

"I see," Glen said and looked down into his lap.

He didn't seem surprised. Was he purposely avoiding eye contact? "I'm sorry," Isaac said sincerely. "We would like you to view the body to confirm that for us." With most of Richie's face missing, Glen would need to use other marks and characteristics to identify him, but Isaac decided not to mention that.

"How did he die?"

"From a gun-shot wound," Isaac answered, purposely omitting the location of the wound. If Glen was responsible for it, he would already know this information, if not, would he ask? Over his years in this line of work, Isaac had found that most family members do. They want to know, was it murder or suicide? If it was murder, do the police have a suspect? In fact, in some cases, the questions were endless.

"His mother will be devastated," was all Glen said.

"My condolences."

Glen nodded, then let out a low growl. "Damn it. I knew this would happen."

"You did?" Isaac asked. "Why?"

Glen rubbed his temple with his fingers. "Because he's a stupid kid. Because he hung around with seedy people. He was a druggie and a gambler. Even as a child he was always up to no good. He never once thought about consequences or how his actions affected others."

Was he pointing fingers or did he have information? Isaac couldn't quite make it out. "Did Richie ever talk about any people he hung around with? Can you give me any names or information for any of them?"

He shook his head. "No," he replied as if that were a very stupid question. He pointed a fat finger toward the window. "They're out there on the streets."

Isaac cocked his head. "He never mentioned any names?"

Glen looked at him like he was crazy. "Hell no. He was down here dealing drugs. These weren't friends. I tried to warn him, but he never listened to me."

Obviously, this was a sore subject. Sore enough that Glen wanted to make it stop? Permanently?

"No! No! No!" Mama wailed from down the hallway. Glen winced at the sound.

Isaac wondered if he had underestimated Mr. Quiddler's age. He looked haggard. "Did he ever mention the name Garrett Holt?"

Isaac could see the wheels turning inside Glen's head. "No," he said. "Was he a drug dealer? Did he kill Richie?"

It wasn't often Isaac could be positive about anything, but this he knew for certain. "No, he didn't kill Richie."

"Well, I've never heard of him."

"Mr. Quiddler, when was the last time you saw Richie?"

"Last Wednesday."

"Did he come over here?"

"He hasn't been here to see his grandmother since before he could drive. I went to his apartment."

"Why were you there?"

"To get my truck."

"Richie had your truck?"

"Yeah." But he sure wasn't going to tell Isaac that Richie had stolen it.

"Did you have a conversation with him?"

"Yeah." He shifted in his chair and pulled his shirt down over his belly.

"Did Richie seem fearful or worried about anything? On edge at all?"

"No." Richie was his usual self — cocky and disrespectful, but Glen wasn't going to tell him that either.

Isaac sighed. These one-word answers were getting him nowhere. "Did he mention anything out of the ordinary? Anything that might help with this investigation?"

"Out of the ordinary? Yes."

Isaac sat up in his seat. *Did he say yes?* "Please, tell me."

This was the opportunity Glen had been waiting for — and no one could tie him to it. "He said he got a job."

"A job?"

"Yes," Glen affirmed. "And Richie told me if they found out he'd told me about it, they'd kill him." He suppressed a smile.

"*They'd* kill him? Who were they?"

"The Rennickes. The younger one. Tucker Rennicke. You may have heard of him; he's running for state representative." Just the mention of that name made his blood boil after all the turmoil they had caused in his life, but the disruption this little revelation would now cause in their empire would bring Glen untold joy. He'd never forget that life-changing moment twenty-five years ago.

♦♦♦

Glen had stepped out the back door with a garbage bag in hand when an unusual sound caught his attention. *What was it? It sounded like crying.* He stopped and listened. Sure enough, and it was coming from the tree house. He set down the bag and walked over to the tree trunk. "Hello?" he called up into the tree. "Who's there?"

The crying stopped.

"I'm coming up. I won't hurt you."

He climbed up the rungs slowly, put his head through the opening in the floorboards and saw her sitting on the pink cushion he had placed in the treehouse three years ago just for her. "Caroline," he said. "What's wrong?"

The tears began again. She couldn't speak. She waved a wad of papers in the air, then threw them to the floor.

He climbed in and picked them up. Across the front of the page in red ink it said 'Confidential.' "May I?" he asked.

She nodded.

He took a moment and skimmed through the document. He looked up at her. "You're pregnant?"

She nodded.

Rodney Rennicke was the father and he was proposing to disclaim all right to the child. The Rennickes would pay Caroline one hundred thousand dollars provided she would agree never to reveal the name of the father of her child to anyone, never speak of her relationship with Rod to anyone, and never come within one hundred yards of any member of the Rennicke family. It was coldblooded. Rod had used her and now he was done with her.

Glen could think of no words to soothe her. "Caroline," he said, and took her in his arms. It wasn't long ago that she was his, but at the beginning of cabin season, she broke it off with him to take up with rich Rod Rennicke. Glen had been devastated.

But here she was. That she came to his treehouse was a sign she felt safe here. Safe with him. Glen's eyes teared up at the thought that this was where she came for solace, for comfort.

She held Glen tight. "He told me he loved me."

Some men will say anything to get a woman in bed. "I know."

She sat back on the cushion. "But he doesn't want me."

She looked so forlorn. Glen took out his handkerchief and wiped the tears from her face. "He's a fool."

She shook her head. "No, Glen. I'm the fool. I never should have left you."

He brushed the hair from her face. "Then stay with me." He took her hands in his. "Caroline, I'm going to ask you the same question I asked you last April." He took a knee. "Caroline, I have loved you since I was ten years old. My feelings for you will never change. Will you marry me?"

The following weekend they tied the knot.

Six months later they brought baby Richard home from the hospital.

Caroline set him in the crib. She looked down lovingly at the newborn and took hold of Glen's hand. "Isn't he beautiful?" Caroline asked.

The words stung. *Beautiful? What did she see?* All Glen saw was the face of Rodney Rennicke staring back at him. Glen tried to get past it, to feel like the better man, the one who came to rescue the maiden from the talons of the beast, but he couldn't. Every time he looked at Richie, he felt sick to his stomach. He hated him.

♦♦♦

"Richie was going to work for Tucker Rennicke?" Isaac asked.

"That's what Richie told me. Very hush-hush," Glen said.

CHAPTER 19

"This can't possibly be right," Petruco said as he burst through the meeting room door with the report in hand looking like a vulture who just lost its prey. "This isn't right," he repeated.

Isaac sat back in his seat. *Here we go.* "What's that Captain?" he asked.

"The gun." Petruco shook the report in the air. "This says it's registered to Tucker Rennicke."

That is indeed what the report said. The report also said they had confirmation Tucker Rennicke's gun was unquestionably the gun used in the murder of Richie Quiddler. They could not, however, make any determination if it was also the weapon used to murder Garrett Holt. But the further they got into these investigations the more Isaac was convinced that the two killings were not related; that it was merely coincidence the two dead bodies were found at the same location. The intel Red was delivering was not finding any street connections either, indicating that was the case.

"That's right," Isaac responded calmly, wondering what had so ruffled Petruco's feathers. In fact, this single fact made all the other pieces regarding Richie's demise start to fall into place. "Perhaps Tucker and Richie weren't such good friends after all."

Petruco stared at Isaac. "They knew each other?"

Tom rolled his eyes.

It was suddenly clear to them what the problem was. Petruco hadn't read the full the report. Obviously, the gun information got him stirred him up for some reason and he didn't read any further. Isaac and Tom would now need to get him up to speed.

"Yes," Isaac answered. "They have known each other since they were children. Tucker's family had a cabin in Richie's hometown."

"In Plummer's Point," Petruco said.

Isaac and Tom shared a look. "That's right," Isaac affirmed.

"I've been there," Petruco said. "Senator Rennicke is a friend of mine." Actually, they weren't exactly friends. They had more of a symbiotic relationship. Petruco supported the senator politically, and in turn, the senator supported Petruco in his career aspirations with the police department. Petruco had attended a fund-raising event held at the senator's cabin.

So that was the problem, Isaac thought to himself. "I see. Well, if you look at my report, a man, who we later learned was Tucker Rennicke, called Richie's cell phone the night he was murdered which is how we tracked Tucker down."

"Are we sure it's the same Tucker Rennicke who is running for state representative?"

"Yes, the same," Isaac confirmed. "I interviewed Tucker on Monday and he told me he had been giving money to Richie to help him with his drug and gambling addictions."

Petruco started to pace. "Giving money to Richie?" he asked.

"Yes."

"Right. Nice people those Rennickes."

Tom bit his lip.

"I'm sure they are, Captain," Isaac said. "But we believe in this case, it was more likely that Richie was blackmailing Tucker."

Petruco stopped and pointed his finger in Isaac's face. "These are fine, upstanding people, Isaac. If the senator's son says he was helping Richie, I'm going to believe him until I have good evidence otherwise."

This was going to be trouble. To get a search warrant, the police had to provide enough evidence to the judge to show they had probable cause. It wasn't often they could produce the gun used in the crime, show a relationship between the parties, and offer a possible motive like they could on this case. But given this last exchange with Petruco, it appeared the Captain's friendship would end up being their biggest hurdle.

"We feel there's enough evidence here to get a warrant to search Tucker Rennicke's house and vehicles," Isaac said.

Petruco did a quick shake of his head. "No, we still have too many questions."

Tom couldn't keep silent any longer. "Questions?"

Petruco trained his raptor eyes on him. "Yes, Wisconsin," he said derisively. He couldn't remember his name, but wouldn't have used it even if he could. "For starters, why would Tucker call Richie that evening if he had killed him that morning?"

"To cover his tracks," Tom answered, then countered with his own question. "What about the gun? It's been proven to be the gun that killed Richie and it's registered to Tucker."

"I don't know," Petruco stammered, then asserted, "It could have been stolen."

Tom stood, ready to make his case, eye to eye and on even ground. "But it was never reported stolen," he said. "And Tucker, out of the goodness of his heart, gave Richie thousands of dollars?" He let out a laugh. "Give me a break."

"Yes. Why not?" Petruco responded. "As Isaac said, they were long-time friends." He pulled out a chair and took a seat in king-like fashion. "You have nothing concrete. We'll need more evidence."

Tom threw up his hands. "Well, how are we going to get more evidence if we can't search his house? And if we don't get there soon, he'll have time to destroy any evidence that may still be there."

"Sit down, Wisconsin," Petruco ordered, then turned his attention to Isaac. "There's got to be other suspects. Who are they?"

"Well yes," Isaac said. "In addition to the bookies and drug dealers, there is one other specific suspect. Richie's father, Mr. Glen Quiddler. The neighbor across the hall heard Mr. Quiddler threaten to kill Richie," he told him. "Tucker Rennicke also said he has heard Mr. Quiddler make similar threats."

Petruco slammed his palms on the table. "Now we're getting somewhere."

Tom dropped into his chair and put his head in his hands just as Red entered waving a piece of paper like it was a flag.

"This just in," Red said. He laid the paper on the table in front of them with a flourish. They all leaned over to view it. "This receipt puts Tucker Rennicke at the restaurant where the bloody clothes and duffle bag were found on that very same day."

Petruco sat back in his seat and pursed his lips. "Could be coincidence. They live nearby, right?"

That last bit of evidence was enough for Petruco to finally agree to begrudgingly request a search warrant. They hoped to have the team at the Rennicke home and ready to start early the next morning.

While waiting for word from the judge, Isaac and Tom decided to take another look at the file. Isaac spread the photos out on his desk, then picked up the one showing the location of the gun when it was spotted by one of the team searching the area. It sat in a cave-like crevice of rocks.

How did it end up there? Isaac wondered. If the killer had thrown it into the woods when fleeing the scene, there would be a one in a thousand chance it would end up in that spot. No, he decided, the killer most likely had purposely placed it there.

Isaac handed the picture showing the gun to Tom. "Do you think Tucker intended to come back for it?"

Before he could answer, Tom's cell phone rang. "Just a sec," he said to Isaac, then went to the hallway to take the call.

Isaac hoped the search warrant would give them the authority to check Tucker's bank records to see just how much money Tucker had given Richie. Tucker must know that there would be a record of it. *Otherwise, why would he admit to that?*

Tom came back ten minutes later holding up his kale and wheat germ salad bowl. "Ready for lunch?"

"Famished. Have a seat." Isaac folded up the file and took his lunch out of the drawer. He opened up the Ziplock bag and removed his ham and cheese sandwich. "So, who was on the phone?"

"Mi profesora de español."

"Oh? Do you have class tonight?"

"No. She offered me a free private lesson."

Isaac smiled. "A private lesson?"

"Yep." Tom set his salad bowl on Isaac's desk. "But I told her I prefer the group classes."

Isaac shook his head. "What is wrong with you?"

Tom pulled up a chair, spun it around and sat straddling it. *Plenty*, he thought to himself, but was not in the mood to share. "What I want to know," he said changing the subject. "Is who went to Richie's apartment that morning."

"And why," Isaac added.

CHAPTER 20

Isaac and Tom had just finished their lunch when Peg popped in the door. She looked like she was going to burst from excitement.

"You're not going to believe this, but there's someone here who wants to confess to murdering Garrett Holt."

Isaac sat back in his chair. "What?"

"You heard me," she said. "It's better than the movies when the killer admits to it all on the witness stand." She squealed. "This guy just walked in the front door to the precinct all by himself."

"Huh. Have an officer put him in the meeting room," Isaac instructed. "And get Red in here, I want him on the other side of the mirror." *Could this be for real?*

"Consider it done," Peg said.

Isaac pointed a finger at her. "And don't let him leave."

"Are you kidding? I'll tell them to lock him up tight," she promised. Maybe now she'd be allowed to wash Red's undercover clothes. She grinned. If this man was Garrett Holt's killer, there was sure to be a celebration at their house tonight.

They assembled as quickly as possible. Red rocketed in he was so pumped. If this was verifiable, he could finally get this monkey off his back. Prior to losing Garrett Holt, he'd been the pride of the undercover division. Since losing Garrett Holt, everyone insisted on saying things like "Don't lose him" and "If he goes to the bathroom, follow him," and "Don't mess this up," and he was getting really tired of it. He needed to prove he was still as good as he ever was.

Red had been doing all he could to identify Garrett's killer, and had instructed the uniformed officers to put pressure on the gambling community to make a scape goat out of whoever that was, because not only the police, but the racketeers as well, had determined the killer was a part of the underground organization. As Red told Isaac earlier, the bookies were seething mad to hear Garrett had been murdered. Losing that huge source of income was a substantial blow to their bottom line. Someone had to pay.

There was no honor among thieves here, it was all about the money.

So, once the bookies determined Lance Spalati was the last to have a "visit" with Garrett, and after Lance reluctantly admitted to causing Garrett's demise (subsequent to some hands on "encouragement"), they gave Lance up like a lamb to the slaughter. Without doubt, Lance's tormentors also threatened his family to further incentivize him to go along. Lance was probably given the not so pleasant alternatives of either watching his family brutalized or murdered, being murdered himself, or, turning himself in to the cops and paying the price through the legal system. At least the last was not lethal. It would be a lesson to any future thugs who overstepped their boundaries. And, by turning him over to the police, it would stop this recent inundation of cops from continuing to snoop around in their business — or at least get things back to the status quo.

Red pulled off his stocking cap letting his red, frizzy hair free and sat next to Petruco in the small room on the viewing side of the one-way mirror.

Petruco squinted at the man on the other side. "You know this guy?"

Red took a breath and let it out slow. "Oh yeah. Bad dude."

Lance Spalati was a strong, stocky man of medium build with dark wavy hair. His driver's license said he was thirty-six years old and lived in Richfield. He had a rap sheet full of minor offenses and a reputation on the street for being brutal. Lance was the one you called when you needed some serious persuasion.

Isaac and Tom entered the room and took the seats opposite Lance with their backs to the glass.

"Whoa," Tom said as he sat down.

Mr. Spalati's face was so bruised, it was hard to match it to the driver's license photo.

"Mr. Spalati, I'm Isaac Scott and this is my partner, Tom Bryant." He did not bother with a handshake. "Are you in need of medical assistance?"

"No," Lance said. "I'm fine."

Lance's right eye was so swollen it looked ready to burst. "Tom, get Mr. Spalati an ice pack," Isaac instructed.

Tom pushed back from the table and left the room.

"You don't look fine. What happened to you?"

"I fell down the stairs."

"It must have been a long flight of stairs," Isaac said. Like from the top of the Empire State Building.

"Yeah," Lance said.

Tom returned with an ice pack and held it out to Lance.

Lance sat defiantly, his hands clasped in his lap.

Tom set it on the table in front of him, then returned to his seat.

Isaac shook his head. *Given he was here to confess to murder, why the tough guy act?* But then he knew he'd never understand the workings of a brain like Spalati's. If that's the way he wanted to play it, there was nothing Isaac could do about it. "I understand you would like to confess to murdering Garrett Holt. Is that correct?"

Lance looked at Isaac with his good eye. "Yeah."

Tom readied his pen. Although they would tape this confession, Tom would take notes of things he noticed, inconsistencies in the story, and questions he thought Isaac should ask.

"Well then, let's get to it," Isaac said.

Lance told them an abbreviated tale of fight or die while Tom scribbled in his notebook. The gash on Lance's lip began to ooze while he spoke.

Isaac pushed a box of tissues toward him. "Let's go over the details, shall we?"

Lance sat stiffly. "Sure."

"So let me get this straight. You picked Garrett up at the coffee shop."

"Right." He licked the blood from his lip.

"Then you drove to Birchwood Park to take a walk."

He nodded.

"In the middle of February."

He shrugged, then gave in, picked up the ice pack, and put it to his eye. "Yeah."

"Was this something you did often? Take walks together?"

He shrugged again. "I don't know." He pulled out a tissue and dabbed his lip.

"You don't know?"

"Okay. Yeah. I guess so." Certainly, his meetings with Garrett became more frequent as Garrett's debt increased.

"So, you were friends?"

"Sure. You could say that." He shifted in his seat and cringed.

He must have broken a few ribs in the "fall" too, Isaac realized. "So then what happened?"

"I already told you," he said. "We were walking, when all of a sudden Garrett got really mad."

"Why was he mad?"

"I don't know." He moved the ice pack to the gash on his forehead and flinched.

"You don't know why he got mad at you?"

"Nah. It's all kind of blurry now. You know, being so traumatic and all," Lance said. "He just got really mad. So he starts slugging me and I keep running away. But then he keeps after me. And he says "I'm going to kill you.""

"He told you he was going to kill you?"

He eased back in his chair and grimaced. "Yeah. Yeah. Lots of times."

"Okay."

"And he's a big dude, so I'm getting, you know, scared and all."

Garrett had been a big man indeed, and Isaac knew from personal experience, Garrett could also be quite hostile and unpredictable.

"So then he starts charging at me and I'm thinking it's either him or me," Lance continued. "So, I shot him. It was total self-defense."

Some details about the case had been kept from the media. Details only the killer would know. "Where did you shoot him?"

"I don't know exactly." Water droplets appeared on his forehead, but it was hard to tell if he was perspiring or if it was condensation from the ice pack. "He was a moving target. I just wanted to stop him is all. Like I said, he was a BIG dude."

"You must have some idea."

"I think it hit him in the stomach 'cause he fell back and grabbed himself there."

That was the right answer and only the perpetrator would know it. All Lance's other subterfuge aside, Isaac actually did believe that Garrett attacked and Lance shot to stop him. It was the rest of Lance's story, or lack thereof, that would be the final nail in his coffin. Nobody would believe that somebody else came along later and covered the body with brush. But Lance knew if he admitted to doing that, his plea of self-defense would be moot. "And then you just left?" Isaac asked.

"Well yeah, but I didn't think he'd just lay there and die. I thought he'd get up and get help."

"After taking a bullet in the stomach?"

"Yeah. Like I say, I didn't shoot to kill him, just to stop him."

"Just so I'm clear, you're saying you shot him and then immediately left the scene. Is that right? That after you shot him you didn't say anything to him or do anything after you shot him?"

"Right." He moved the ice pack back over his eye. "I just wanted to get out of there. He could have gotten up and come after me again."

"After being shot in the stomach."

He shifted in his seat again and winced. "Yeah. I'm telling you, this guy was crazy. It was total self-defense."

From all reports, Isaac knew this would be a waste of time, but Petruco had insisted. "Now tell me about Richie Quiddler."

"Who?"

"Richie Quiddler."

"I don't know a Richie Quiddler." He moved the ice pack to the side of his neck.

"Richie Quiddler was shot at Birchwood Park just yards from where Garrett was found. Did you take a walk with him too?"

"Hey, don't try to pin that on me. I don't know nothin' about it." He looked nervous for the first time since their meeting began. "I should probably get a lawyer."

CHAPTER 21

Captain Petruco paced back and forth in front of his mahogany desk. "Well Pop, I've got good news and bad news," he said to the man in the photo on the wall.

"First, the good news," the Captain said. "Remember the one who slipped our tail last February and we found dead in Birchwood Park a couple of weeks ago? Well, it turns out, he was a regular and exhaustive source of funds to the bookmakers, and they were not happy to hear that this particular source of income had been terminated. They were even more unhappy to learn the one responsible for this loss of revenue stream was one of their own." He puffed up his chest. "Our undercover team really put the pressure on those bookmakers, and in turn those thugs put the pressure on the killer. So much so that he actually walked right into the station to confess." He gave a high five to the photograph. "It was just plain astounding."

"But . . ." He put a hand to his forehead and took a deep breath. "We've got big, big trouble with that second murder," Petruco said. "The son of one of our senators, a senator I've endorsed for years, is being investigated for the murder. Not only that, but the son is also running for office and I've donated money to both of their campaigns."

He crossed his arms over his chest. "I'm between a rock and a hard place on this one. If I don't investigate the son, the press will accuse me of partiality, prejudice, partisanship, and all those other politically charged "P" words. If I do investigate the son, the senator will turn on me and my career may be on the line."

He moved to the other side of the desk and opened the bottom drawer. He took out the bottle of Jack Daniels and poured a shot. "I tried my best to put in a good defense of the kid, but it all fell flat." He picked up the shot glass and threw it down in one gulp. "Tell me this, will you? Why should I have to pay the price for this kid's deed?"

The telephone rang, interrupting his diatribe. "Captain Petruco," he answered.

"The judge can see you in half an hour," the voice on the other end of the line said.

Petruco hung up the phone and stood in front of the photo. "I gotta go see the judge, Pop, and ask for a search warrant. The only thing that may save my ass, is that I know the judge supports the senator too, so I'm not alone in this."

♦♦♦

Glen paced back and forth across the floor of Richie's empty apartment; his footsteps echoing off the walls. He was going to have to make the call, and he didn't want to. But he'd put it off long enough. He needed that truck back. He rubbed his forehead. Worry filled his eyes. *Who knows what they found inside?* He wrung his hands. *Incriminating stuff?* Maybe it was best to let sleeping dogs lie.

He did an about face. If they had found anything, you'd think they would have contacted him by now. *Yes, certainly they would have contacted him by now.* He and his truck needed to get back to Plummer's Point and far away from here. The shop was in chaos and his wife was in mourning. He took out his cell phone and dialed.

It was answered on the first ring. "Detective Scott."

"Yeah, Detective. This is Glen Quiddler, Richie's dad," he said. "I'm wondering when I can get my truck back."

Isaac blinked. "Your truck?"

"Yeah." Glen tugged on the old sheet that still covered the window. "It looks like they're done here at Richie's apartment, so I'd like to pack the truck and go home."

Richie still had his truck? "I'm sorry, Mr. Quiddler, I thought you said you picked it up from Richie last Wednesday."

Glen scratched his bald head. "No, I said I went there to pick it up. But Richie said he needed it for his job, so I let him keep it."

"For his job? The job for Tucker Rennicke?" *How could he have missed that?*

"Yeah. The job for Tucker Rennicke."

"Mr. Quiddler, I don't believe you mentioned that."

"Oh?"

"Mr. Quiddler, we don't have your truck."

The police didn't have it? "Well, it's not here in the parking lot."

Isaac pressed his lips together. Why hadn't it occurred to him that Richie had to have some way to get to Birchwood Park that morning? "We'll find it for you Mr. Quiddler."

"Thanks," Glen said, then let his forehead fall against the wall. What can of worms did he just open? Why didn't he just leave this alone?

"What's the license plate number?" Isaac asked.

Tom returned from Petruco's office just as Isaac ended the call.

"Hey Jefe, did you know Petruco talks to that picture on his wall?"

Isaac tore the page off the note pad. "Yeah, it's his dad. He was a sergeant on the force and was killed in the line of duty. I wouldn't mention it."

Sergeant Petruco had been an exemplary cop. From all reports he was on his way to the top, but was killed in his prime leaving behind his wife and teenage son. A son who vowed to continue his father's legacy.

"Huh, I didn't know that," Tom said. "That helps explain some things." Tom knew first-hand how hard it was to lose a loved one. Some people never got past it. If it helped Petruco to have conversations with a photograph, Tom would be the last one to criticize.

"Very tragic. Petruco was just a kid."

They stood in silence for a minute. The possibility of being killed in the line of duty was always at the back of every officer's mind.

Tom noticed the paper in Isaac's hand. "What do you have there?"

"Remember Glen Quiddler's truck?"

"The one Richie had?"

"Yes. Well, Mr. Quiddler told me he went to get it from Richie that day, but what he neglected to mention was that he *didn't* get it."

"What?"

"He left it with Richie for the job for Tucker Rennicke. Richie still had it."

Tom hit his forehead with the palm of his hand. "And we better find it."

"Right." Isaac pointed at the envelope in Tom's hand. "Did Petruco get the search warrant?"

Tom held it up for Isaac to see. "Right here."

"Excellent. Does it include bank records?"

"Yep." Tom laid the envelop on Isaac's desk. "Let's just hope all the physical evidence hasn't already been destroyed."

"No kidding."

Tom's cell phone pinged. "Ugh," he said.

"What's up?"

"My spin instructor wants my feedback on her class."

"So?"

"I already sent it to her in a text."

Isaac grinned. "Did it ever occur to you that she wants more than just feedback?"

"Yeah." Tom stepped toward the door. "But's that all I have for her." He gave a wave. "I'm off to my axe throwing tournament."

"Axe throwing?" Isaac shook his head. "Please be careful."

"No worries, Jefe. It's all very safe. See you bright and early tomorrow."

Spanish. Spin class. Axe throwing. Was there anything he didn't do? No wonder he didn't have time for women. Isaac picked up the phone. "Peg," he said. "I need you to get an APB out for a truck," he told her. "It's urgent."

CHAPTER 22

Tom was early for class so he parked at the far end of the lot under a maple tree. He moved his seat back and pushed the disc into the player. The sound of Mozart Concerto No. 3 filled the car. He closed his eyes and listened, patiently counting out the stanza's, waiting for the violin solo. And there it was. Tears came to his eyes. Even before, this one always made him cry. He took the photo out of his wallet and held it to his heart. How he missed her.

She had been the soloist for this number the first time he saw her. He was so enraptured, he lingered after the concert to try to get an autograph. She emerged, he handed her his pen, and felt an immediate connection. "Would you add a telephone number too?" he had asked, and was overjoyed when she did.

He had barely been able to wait twenty-four hours before calling her.

And it took all the patience he could muster to wait until the anniversary of their first date before asking for her hand. He was elated when she miraculously said yes, and he couldn't help but marvel at his good fortune.

It was just over a year now since the last time Tom saw her. It was the night they all gathered at her family's church for the wedding rehearsal.

For some reason, he always remembered it in slow motion. He had taken his position at the front of the church, with his brother by his side, while her friends from the orchestra tuned up. His parents smiled at him from the front pew. Her mother blew him a kiss, then turned toward her husband and daughter at the back of the sanctuary. The pastor behind the pulpit nodded for the music to begin and the melodious sounds of *Canon in D* came forth. Tom watched spellbound as she glided down the aisle on the arm of her father, as if she were on a cushion of air. He would never forget the way she looked coming toward him. Like an angel. He wished he could have married her right then and there.

The rehearsal was followed by the groom's dinner with toasts of good wishes for their new life together and the clanging of spoons against water glasses, insisting they kiss. How he had loved her.

He walked her to her car. "Samantha, can't I please come stay with you tonight?"

"Absolutely not," she said. "It's bad luck for the groom to see the bride before the wedding."

She gave him a kiss and drove off.

He and his brother arrived at the church the next day with garment bags in hand. They were directed to the back lavatory where the groomsmen would be getting ready.

On the way, they were to pass the church library where the bridesmaids were having their hair done.

"Close the door," Tom called as they approached. "Groom coming through, and I'm not allowed to see the bride before the wedding."

Amber, Samantha's sister and the maid of honor, peaked out nervously. "Hey Tom," she said, but decided not to tell him that Samantha, who was supposed to be there an hour earlier, had not yet arrived. The girls had been trying to reach her, but Samantha hadn't answered any of their calls. Now learning that she was not with Tom, made Amber even more concerned. She watched Tom enter the lavatory, then slipped out of the room in search of her mother. Amber found her in the sanctuary directing the florist.

"Mom, have you heard from Samantha?"

She furrowed her brow. "Isn't she with you?"

Amber shook her head.

Her mother looked at her watch. "Well, there's still plenty of time. Maybe she decided to find some different shoes. I know she wasn't completely happy with the ones she had."

"The hairdresser is just about done with everybody else."

"Did you call her?"

"Yes, many times. But she's not answering."

Her mother reached over and gently straightened one of the curls on the side of Amber's face. "She must have turned the ringer off like she does for concerts. I'm sure she'll show up soon. Try to get the hairdresser to hang on longer. Tell her I'll pay for her time."

"Okay."

She watched her daughter walk away, then ran toward the back of the church to find her husband. "Darren! Darren!"

Darren set down the programs when he saw her coming. He knew that look. "What's wrong, dear?"

She wrung her hands. "Samantha isn't here yet. Would you please go check her apartment?"

He nodded and checked his trousers for his keychain.

Darren returned forty-five minutes later to find his wife pacing anxiously. "There was no clue as to where she might be?"

He shook his head. He had looked through her apartment, and while he was glad he didn't find her there in some dire situation, or see any evidence of a struggle or crime, he had been hoping to find a note that might explain why she wasn't there today. It wasn't like Samantha to be inconsiderate of other people's feelings, and Samantha would know there were a lot of feelings to consider today. "She still isn't here?"

She shook her head. "Where could she be? Samantha is never late for anything." She pointed to the sanctuary. "Guests are being seated. The service is to start in fifteen minutes."

Darren took his wife gently by the shoulders. "We need to tell Tom. Maybe she mentioned something to him."

Tears came to her eyes. "Yes. I think we have to."

They waited for half an hour, but Samantha never showed up and they weren't able to reach her by phone, so they told the guests to go home.

"She didn't come," Tom said.

"I'm sure there's a good reason," his brother said. "Something must have happened to her."

Tom knew he was trying to cheer him up, but the thought that something happened to her that prevented her from being there today made him worry even more. Was that better than believing she decided not to marry him? Was it better to believe that she was in some kind of trouble, instead of believing that she ran off to avoid the wedding?

After the church was empty, Tom drove to her apartment. Her car was not there. He opened the door and stood in the dark entry. "Samantha?" he called. He switched on the lights and walked from room to room. He opened up closets and looked behind chairs. He looked under the bed and behind the shower curtain. He didn't see her purse, and the suitcase that had been on the floor of the bedroom two days ago wasn't there either. Had she been packing for a honeymoon or an escape? There was no trace of her. Tom sat on the floor and sobbed. It was over an hour later he found the strength to get up and leave her apartment.

Samantha's parents filed a missing person's report with the police, and her disappearance was being reported on all the local news stations. But, because there was no sign of disturbance at her apartment, her car was missing, her purse was missing, her suitcase was missing, and she didn't show up in any accident reports or hospitals in the area, the general consensus of the community, and many of Tom's friends on the police force, was that she got cold feet on her wedding day.

Two days passed with no word. Tom sat and stared at the wall in his apartment trying to remember everything Samantha ever said to him; trying to find some clue that would explain her disappearance.

On the third day, the police received a report of a car at the bottom of a ravine off the rural highway that led to Samantha's apartment. It had rolled below an overpass shielding it from view. There they found Samantha inside, lifeless. The police also discovered the shattered carcass of a deer on their descent down the hillside, leading them to believe it was the cause of the accident.

The most tragic news, however, was that had they found Samantha within the first twenty-four hours, she may have survived. The heart-wrenching reality of this ate away at Tom, filling him with debilitating regret. If only he had called her to wish her a good night's sleep after the groom's dinner. If only he had noticed the dead deer down the embankment when he drove to her apartment after the wedding was called off. If only he had immediately gone out searching for her instead of wallowing in his own sadness. If only, if only, if only. Tom just couldn't get past the knowledge that at the time he was happily preparing for the wedding, Samantha was struggling for her life.

After a year of therapy, Tom decided he would need to make some major changes if he had any chance of getting on with his life. So with that goal in mind, he made the move to Minneapolis. It was also the reason for his need of constant diversions and his nightly use of a sleeping aid.

Fortunately, the painfulness of the ordeal was becoming less and less as time wore on. Tom now cherished the memories of the time he had shared with Samantha, when not long ago those memories had only produced grief. Each day brought new healing, but there were still many emotions yet to work through.

♦♦♦

The days were getting warmer and longer as they moved further into the spring. Isaac rolled down the windows to let the stale air out and the fresh air blow through the car as he drove home.

Tonight was Isaac's turn to prepare dinner and he picked a family favorite: tacos. By the time he got home, Claudia had already set the fixings out for him and was rinsing the tomatoes. Isaac put the hamburger in the fry pan on the stove, and then took out the cutting board and started chopping.

Avery pulled the plates down from the cupboard.

Jacob burst through the back door into the kitchen with a big grin. "You really threw John Rogers' game off today," he said to Avery. "The coach had to put him on the bench."

Isaac stopped chopping onion.

Claudia turned off the faucet and grabbed a towel.

Avery set the plates on the dinner table. "Now how could I do that? I wasn't even there."

Jacob, their middle child who usually liked nothing more than driving his older sister crazy, dropped his back pack on the floor near the door and gave her a friendly punch on the arm. "It was hilarious!" he exclaimed. "When Rogers came onto the court, all the girls started going 'wah, 'wah, 'wah like from 'The Wheels on the Bus.'"

"The wheels on the bus?" Isaac asked.

"Yeah, the song," Jacob explained. Then he started singing, "the wheels on the bus go round and round, round and round,"

Claudia joined in from the sink, "Round and round. The wheels on the bus go round and round."

Isabelle heard the singing and ran into the kitchen to join in. "All round the town," and then they continued the song all together, "The babies on the bus go 'wah, 'wah, 'wah; 'wah, 'wah, 'wah; 'wah, 'wah, 'wah, the babies on the bus go 'wah, 'wah, 'wah all round the town," taking their fists and twisting them by their eyes like babies do when they cry.

Avery snickered at them. "Okay, now that's enough."

Isabelle didn't listen. She was having too much fun. "The mommies on the bus go sh! sh! sh!" She put her pointer finger to her lips. "Sh! sh! sh!, sh! sh! sh!"

"Why did they do that?" Isaac asked, referring to the girls at the basketball game.

"'Cause Avery told everybody she slapped John Rogers and he cried like a baby." Jacob laughed out loud. He had heard the rumors spread around about his big sister, and he didn't like it. It was about time that cocky John Rogers got put in his place.

"I didn't tell EVERYBODY," she said. "Just a few friends. I don't know how everybody else heard about it."

"You slapped him?" Claudia asked.

Avery nodded. "And I don't want to talk about it."

Isaac grinned. *She slapped him.* "That's my girl!"

CHAPTER 23

Isaac and Tom showed up at the door with the search warrant in hand. The sun was just peeking over the horizon making the dew covering the grass glisten. Several police vehicles lined the avenue with crews ready to search the large Tudor home. The reasons for starting first thing in the morning were three-fold. First, to be as certain as possible the residents would be home; second, to minimize the possibility the residents had any prior warning of this visit; and third, to start a task that would most likely take all day. And given the size of the house and depending on what they found, it could even take several days.

Tom rang the bell and then stepped back next to Isaac.

Nikki opened the door with bike helmet in hand. "What's all this?" she asked as she took in the scene.

Isaac held out the search warrant. "Mrs. Rennicke, we are here to search your home."

She turned from the door and hollered, "Tucker, get here quick."

"What's this all about?" she asked Isaac. "Is there someone on the loose?"

Before Isaac could answer, Tucker arrived at the door with his partially buttoned shirt hanging out of his pants. He stuck his head out the door and looked back and forth. "What the hell is this?"

Isaac handed him the search warrant. "We have a warrant to search your home, Mr. Rennicke."

He shoved his glasses up his nose with his middle finger. "No, no I don't think so. You hold on right there." He took his cell phone out of his pocket and hit the speed dial. "Perry, the police are here with a warrant to search my house."

Isaac heard an exclamation of surprise on the other end.

"Yes," Tucker answered. "Yes, I'll take a picture of it and send it to you."

Tucker held the warrant up against the door, photographed it, and then sent it off while Isaac and Tom stood on the step.

There was no need for Isaac to argue with him about it, Tucker would have to let them in. This warrant gave them the right to search the entire single-family home and the vehicles inside it.

Tucker's phone rang. "Yes?" he said impatiently to the caller.

They waited while the caller explained the situation to him.

"This is crap." Tucker snarled, then hung up the phone and glowered at Isaac.

"Perhaps you and Mrs. Rennicke would be more comfortable accompanying me to my office while the crew gets to work, and we can talk about it there," Isaac suggested.

"I'm not leaving," Tucker said.

A Fox 9 news van passed slowly by, followed by a crew from WCCO. Tucker's bulging eyes widened. Panic set in. "Get in here, get in here," he said to Isaac and Tom.

Isaac and Tom entered the home and Tucker swiftly closed the door behind them.

"What the hell is this?" he said again.

"Let's go sit down and let the crew get to work," Isaac said calmly. "The sooner they start the sooner they'll be finished."

They all went back into the kitchen and sat around the granite center island. Tom and Isaac on one side, and Tucker and Nikki on the other.

"How in the world did you get a search warrant?" Tucker asked as he hastily buttoned up his shirt.

"The gun that killed Richie Quiddler is registered to you, Mr. Rennicke."

"What?"

He looked genuinely shocked. Was he that good of an actor?

Tucker pushed the horn-rimmed glasses up his nose with his middle finger. "I didn't kill Richie. I was helping him."

That defense would get him nowhere, but Isaac wasn't going to tell him that. It was difficult to believe that Tucker was giving Richie money so that Richie could buy himself out of trouble — particularly after learning that Rennicke owned the gun that killed him. As Tom suggested, it made much more sense that Tucker was giving Richie money because Richie was blackmailing him.

"Detective," Nikki interjected. "This is crazy. Tucker would never kill anyone." She gave her husband a playful slap across his arm. "I mean, he couldn't even shoot a deer when it stood right in front of him." And that was a fact. She'd never forget the time her father took Tucker out on a hunting trip to 'get to know him.' Tucker was completely out of his element in the cold woods having to sit quietly in a tree stand while his breath fogged up his glasses. Her father said it was like having a little girl with him, and that's when he dubbed Tucker the 'sissy citiot.'

"That's right," Tucker agreed.

"I don't think he even has bullets for that gun," she added. She turned toward Tucker. "Do you have bullets?"

He shot her a look. "I didn't kill Richie," he repeated.

They sat in uncomfortable silence for a moment. Isaac decided to let it linger. He may get more information initially by just letting them talk. Because in reality, they didn't have to answer his questions, and he didn't want to alienate them from the get go.

Nikki sat straighter in her chair, then slammed a fist on the counter. "It must have been stolen," she said to Isaac. She turned toward Tucker. "Damn it, Tucker, how many times did I tell you not to leave that garage door open?" She turned toward Tom. "He leaves it wide open when he mows the lawn. Anyone could have gone right in and taken anything."

"Yes, that's right." Tucker liked that idea. "It must have been stolen."

"You should check to see if anything else is missing," Nikki added. "Maybe they could dust for prints or whatever while they're here and find out who took it."

"Sure," Tom said. "Where did you keep it?"

Tucker kicked Nikki under the counter. "Just shut up," he said to her. "You're not helping."

She shifted in her seat and drummed her brightly polished nails on the countertop.

"My lawyer is on his way," Tucker said.

♦♦♦

Perry Gronholz came inside and examined the search warrant. "Is my client under arrest?" he asked Isaac.

"No, sir."

"Fine, then they will be coming with me." Perry turned toward Tucker. "Tuck in your shirt and walk tall," he instructed. Nikki pulled a jacket over her spandex and picked up her purse. Perry led them past the crew searching the yard while the TV crews filmed the scene. It wouldn't do any good to try to hide their identities. It was public knowledge who owned this property.

Isaac and Tom stood in the doorway as Tucker and Nikki ducked into the back seat. Dark clouds began to move in blocking out the sun as it rose higher in the sky.

"Hope it doesn't rain," Isaac said.

They watched as Perry's Town Car pushed through the crowd of reporters taking Tucker and Nikki away from the scene.

"Hope he doesn't hit anybody," Tom said.

Isaac couldn't help but chuckle. "Let's go and let the forensics team get their work done."

They walked down the front steps and onto the driveway just as the neighbor's car backed out of his garage.

"Stop!" Frank called. "I recognize you," he said to Isaac. "What's all this trouble about?" he asked as though Isaac was the cause.

Isaac took a breath and internally counted to three. "Let me introduce myself," he said. "I'm Detective Isaac Scott with the Minneapolis Police Department and I'd like to ask you a few questions."

Frank looked closely at the badge, then at Isaac's face, then at Tom, then back at Isaac. "Not until I know what this is about," he said, as if he had the right to know.

Isaac put the badge away. "I understand your concern," Isaac responded politely, but ignored his demand for an explanation. "Do you recall seeing a vehicle leaving these premises around 3:30 or 4:00 the morning of Friday, May 15?"

"No. I'm asleep at that time of the night." Frank watched nervously as some of the crew cordoned off the Rennicke's house. *What was happening?*

"Do you recall seeing a vehicle return later that same morning?"

"Return? No." His eyes followed some other crew members carrying equipment into the house. In his own neighborhood? *It was an outrage.* "I saw Tucker leave for work and Nikki go off on her bike ride at 8 a.m. just like every day."

So often people get used to a routine and one day runs into the next. "Just to confirm, this was Friday, May 15?" Isaac asked.

"Yes, I heard you," Frank responded curtly. "The morning of the fifteenth." He looked in his rearview mirror at the television crews setting up their cameras along the street. *Criminals living right next door? This was scandalous.* "What did they do?"

"I am not at liberty to discuss the matter."

Frank knew what that meant. *They had to be stopped.* "I have a security camera hidden in the light fixture over there. You're welcome to view the footage," he told Isaac. He had never liked the Rennickes anyway.

CHAPTER 24

Perry Gronholz's office was on the forty-ninth floor in the IDS Tower, the tallest building in downtown Minneapolis. On a clear day, through the windows of his corner office, Perry could see a breathtaking view of the Minneapolis and suburban landscape that went on for miles and miles. On a windy day, however, the building would sway a bit, oftentimes shortening the work day for the skittish; Perry usually being one of the first to take their leave.

Perry led Tucker and Nikki to a meeting room and instructed his assistant to get them coffee and whatever else they needed while he made some calls. "I'll be back shortly," he assured them.

"How are you going to explain this, Tucker?" Nikki exclaimed the minute the meeting room door closed. "First I find out you're giving Richie Quiddler money, then he shows up dead, and now the police are searching our house. What the hell is happening?"

"I don't know."

"Don't give me that bullshit."

"It's like I said. Richie showed up asking for money saying he was going straight. He's a good friend, so I helped him out."

Good friend? Helping him out? It was laughable. The only reason Tucker was friendly with Richie was because, as a kid, Richie was his source of drugs. Even then, Tucker always took advantage of Richie.

She remembered one time in particular, the summer after her junior year, just after the Fourth of July celebration at Lake Roosevelt.

♦♦♦

It was still ninty degrees even though the sun had set hours ago. Nikki, Tucker and Richie had lingered for a while after the fireworks were done, waiting for the hoards to leave, while drinking beer and getting high around a campfire by the shore.

When Nikki realized it was almost midnight, she jumped up in a panic. "Sorry, boys, I've got to go." She'd be grounded for sure if her dad discovered how late she came home.

"Wait," Richie said. "I'll walk you home." He stood and sprinkled some sand into the firepit to douse the fire. "I'm going that way too."

Tucker looked up at them, slugged down the rest of his tenth beer and rose unsteadily to his feet. "Party poopers," he said. He tottered over to Nikki and gave her a slobbery kiss.

Richie grimaced at the sight. "Gross," he said.

Nikki pushed Tucker back and steadied him as best she could. "Okay, lover boy, it's time to get home," she told him. She pulled a flashlight from her backpack and turned it on. "Here, take this with you."

Nikki and Richie watched as Tucker staggered down the long dirt road to his log fortress, the flashlight scanning the woods erratically.

"He's super drunk," Richie said.

"You think?" Nikki replied sarcastically.

"Hope he doesn't scare a skunk," Richie said, but didn't mean it.

Nikki laughed at the thought. "Come on, let's go."

They walked across the main road, past the grocery store, towards Nikki's house.

Richie pulled the wad of cash Tucker gave him out of his jean pocket and counted. "Shit. He shorted me," he said. "Can you believe it? That son of a bastard, Tucker, has money up the wazoo, and he still cheats. He's the stingiest shit I've ever known."

Nikki shook her head. "Then why do you hang out with him if you hate him so much?"

He shrugged. "Looking for opportunities."

"Opportunities for what?"

He shoved her playfully on the shoulder. "Why do *you* hang out with him?"

She laughed. "That's easy. He's my ticket out of here."

He bumped her with his hip. "You don't belong with him," he said.

♦♦♦

How could Tucker think anyone would believe he was selflessly helping Richie? It was preposterous. And Nikki knew very well that Tucker didn't do anything unless it was for Tucker's own benefit.

She put her hands on her hips and looked him in the eyes. "Oh sure," she said. "I believe you were helping him." She used her fingers to make air quotations around the word 'helping.' "Helping him keep his mouth shut about some of your childhood antics."

Tucker's bulging eyes bulged further. He pushed the glasses up his nose with his middle finger. He could feel the beads of sweat forming on his forehead. If anyone knew of his childhood antics, it was Nikki. "You wouldn't tell about that, would you?" he said.

He looked so forlorn. If he didn't get out of this, his reputation would be ruined. "No," she agreed. "I wouldn't. My lips are sealed."

♦♦♦

It didn't take long before the reports of the search started coming in, and the evidence was overwhelming.

"Can you believe this guy?" Tom asked no one in particular. "It's like he didn't think he'd get caught."

A copious amount of dried blood was found in the trunk of the Mercedes. The lab tests hadn't come back yet, but they all assumed it would be Richie's. Granted, it was initially hard to see given the dark interior, but the luminol they sprayed inside reacted to the iron in the hemoglobin and lit it up like blue Christmas lights.

Petruco paced back and forth in the meeting room like a pendulum target at the state fair shooting gallery.

"I mean, get a load of these pictures," Tom continued.

Under the carpet below the car's front seat they found an envelope stamped *Glen's Gas and Garage* containing photos of a young Tucker doing various illegal and unsavory things. Several showed him smoking a joint, one showed him sucking in a line of what appeared to be cocaine, and a few showed him shirtless, wearing war paint and a feather headdress dancing around a campfire. The most embarrassing photos showed him naked in various pornographic poses.

Petruco punched his right fist into his left palm and plod heavy-footed toward the door, then did an about face and lumbered back to the other side of the room. His mind was reeling.

Isaac sat at the table and examined Tucker's bank records. "From what I can determine, it looks like Tucker paid Richie two hundred fifty grand over the last month."

The search warrant had also allowed them to get into Richie's cell phone which showed that Tucker and Richie had been in steady contact for three weeks prior to Richie's demise. "Let's try to match those payment dates up with the phone calls," Red suggested.

"Excellent idea," Isaac said. "Here's the list of payments," he handed it across the table to Red. "I'm going to go see if IT was able to enhance the footage from Frank's videocam." The footage clearly showed Tucker's car exiting the garage at 3:45 a.m. and returning at 5:35 a.m., but because of the distance of the vehicle from the camera, they hadn't yet been able to confirm who was behind the wheel.

Petruco's hands went to his head. This wasn't looking good for the Rennickes. Tucker might be able to explain away where he went early that morning and the reason for the telephone calls and payments to Richie. The damaging photos didn't need to see the light of day. But why was there blood in the trunk? He would certainly wait for the results of the blood test to confirm it was the victim's blood before arresting Tucker, but if it was a match, he really didn't see any alternative.

Petruco didn't have to wait long. Just as Isaac stood to leave, Joyce from forensics stuck her head in the door.

"Hey men," she said. "We got the results back."

Petruco stood stock still.

"It's a match," she said. "The blood in the trunk belonged to Richie Quiddler."

Tom smiled. "We've got him now."

Petruco threw up his hands. "I have no choice." He left the room without a further word.

◆◆◆

Isaac and the uniformed officers took the elevator up to Perry Gronholz's office on the forty-ninth floor. The receptionist greeted them and instructed them to wait in the lobby.

Perry and Tucker appeared ten minutes later with Nikki in tow.

Tucker looked shell shocked.

One of the officers read Tucker his rights and placed him under arrest.

"But I'm innocent," Tucker said as they put the cuffs on. "Perry, aren't you going to do anything?"

Perry turned toward Isaac. "I want to see the evidence immediately."

"I can't go to jail," Tucker wailed.

"We'll have the evidence for you at the station," Isaac said to Perry.

"I didn't kill Richie," Tucker squealed.

"No one speaks to my client unless I am present, is that understood?" Perry put a hand on Tucker's shoulder. "We'll arrange for bail."

The officers led Tucker to the elevator bank and pushed the down arrow. Tucker looked stupefied.

Was Tom right? Isaac wondered. *Was Tucker so bold that he never expected to get caught? Or was it something else?* Tucker's surprise at learning of Richie's death when Isaac first interviewed him had seemed genuine, but then why had Tucker been paying Richie? Isaac rubbed the back of his neck. What was he missing? He studied Tucker's face as he stood in the elevator, and ultimately decided that Tucker didn't look bold, he looked cornered.

Nikki stood inside the lobby door and waved to Tucker. "I'm here, Tuck," she called out.

"This can't be happening," Tucker said as the elevator door closed.

They rode down in silence. That nagging feeling Isaac sometimes called a hunch tugged at him. *Something was definitely missing.* As they placed Tucker in the car, Isaac leaned in and inserted his business card into the front pocket of Tucker's shirt. "Let me know when you're ready to confess."

Tucker glared at him. "I told you, I didn't kill Richie Quiddler."

"I believe that," Isaac said. But Isaac knew there had to be more to the story that only Tucker could tell him now.

CHAPTER 25

Tucker had been in custody for less than fourteen hours, but that was plenty of time to scrutinize all the evidence and consider his circumstance many times over. The prosecutor hadn't filed the charges yet, but it sounded like they could come down any second.

On Tucker's request, Tucker, Nikki and Perry Gronholz assembled in one of the meeting rooms for a private conference after Perry and his team had examined and re-examined all of Tucker's defense options. To Perry's dismay, given the evidence the police had obtained, they couldn't find any that would hold any water. The last resort was always the insanity plea, and in this case, it appeared to be their only alternative.

Tucker pushed the glasses back up his nose. "How does it look?" he asked his attorney, even though he already knew the answer.

"I'm sorry Tuck, but I must be honest," Perry said. "It doesn't look good. The evidence is strong and irrefutable. It was your gun. Your car pulled out of the garage prior to the murder, and pulled back in after the time of the murder. The victim's blood was found in your trunk, you visited the restaurant where the bloody duffle bag of clothes was found on that day, and most people will doubt that you'd give two hundred fifty grand to the victim just to help him out." He sighed. "Especially since the discovery of the damaging photographs."

Tucker shifted in his seat.

"The victim was shot from behind, so it would be hard to argue self-defense," Perry continued. He took a deep breath and readied himself to deliver the bad news. "I think we'll be looking at a charge of first-degree murder."

Nikki reached over and took Tucker's hand. It was cold. He was done for.

Tucker nodded resignedly. "I need a minute to speak with my wife. Privately, please."

Perry stood and pushed in his chair. "I'll be just outside the door."

Tucker and Nikki watched him leave.

As soon as the door closed Tucker pulled his hand away from hers. "So, how did you find out?" he asked her.

"Find out?"

"That I hired Richie to kill you."

She sat back in her seat. "What?"

"Did you find out about my payments to him through bank statements somehow?"

She looked around nervously. "Tucker?"

"Did you snoop at my cell messages?"

"Tucker. Quiet down. Someone might be listening."

"It's just you and me here, Nikki."

"Are you sure?"

"Do you see anyone else?"

She shook her head. "No, but . . ."

He pushed the glasses up his nose with his middle finger. "I just want to know where I went wrong."

"You're actually telling me that you hired Richie to kill me?"

He stood abruptly. "Did you have me followed?" He placed his hands on the back of the chair. "And where did those pictures come from?"

"You're in the pictures and you don't remember?" He was unraveling right before her eyes.

He started to pace. "You must have arranged for this prior to that morning, because otherwise why would you have been wearing my hunting gear? And taken my gun? And driven my car? I just can't figure out what went wrong." He wrung his hands. "It was a perfect plan."

Perfect plan?

He circled the table in a clockwise direction. "It was almost handed to me on a platter." He held out his right hand. "Here I've got Richie, a natural born hoodlum, who worshipped me, and . . ." He held out the other hand. "Who desperately needed money."

"No. No," she interrupted him. "You're all wrong there. Richie would have liked nothing better than to stick it to you."

He abruptly changed direction. "Richie followed me around like a loyal dog."

"You're so full of yourself. Richie only wanted your money."

He stopped and pounded his chest. "Richie idolized me. Richie wanted to *be* me."

She rolled her eyes. "He played you. All the time. And you ate it up."

"Played me?" he gaffed. "Well, he hated you." He narrowed his eyes at her. "Is that why you did it?"

"Seriously? Richie has loved me since the second grade. He'd never hurt me."

"Oh, I think you're mistaken, there. I hate to tell you this, but he never had a nice word to say about you. In fact, I won't even repeat the things he did say about you."

"You are such a rube. He just didn't want *you* to like me."

He froze in place. *Could I have been so wrong?* His hands flew to his head. "So, that's it. Richie told you."

"Really? You hired *Richie* to kill me?" She laughed. "What in the world were you thinking?"

He pushed the glasses up his nose with his middle finger. "I thought I'd turn a liability into an advantage."

"A liability?"

"Yes. You're unpredictable, crude — a wild card. But dead, you were my trump card. Suddenly, everyone would like me, feel sorry for me, want to help me. I'd win the election in a heartbeat."

"Bonehead move, Tuck."

"So, you admit it. You shot Richie."

"I admit nothing. But isn't it nice that it only took one bullet to destroy two bastards?"

♦♦♦

Isaac received the call an hour later. "Tucker Rennicke says he's ready to confess."

CHAPTER 26

Nikki should have realized that he'd figure it out, but Tucker's admission that he hired Richie to kill her scared her to the core. She knew how vindictive he could be. It seemed inevitable that he would now turn the tables on her. But, if it came down to her word against his, at least she had the damaging photographs on her side. She was now very glad she took the time to stop by the shop and sneak the envelope from Glen's garage when they visited last weekend. The prosecutors would need to prove a motive, and the pictures, contained in the envelope from Richie's dad's garage were the physical evidence to prove Tucker had one.

It seemed like an eternity, but it was only two weeks ago Richie was waiting for her on the front stoop when she returned from her afternoon bike excursion.

♦♦♦

"Look what the cat dragged in," she had said to him.

"Happy to see you, too, Nikki." Richie flicked his cigarette onto the grass adding it to the sixteen others. *She looked just the same as she did in high school*, he thought to himself. *Maybe even better.*

Richie Quiddler on her front step. *This could only be trouble.* "Why are you here?" she asked. She hadn't seen him since the night before her wedding four years ago.

He stood and stretched. "To let you know your husband called me."

She entered the garage door code, careful to make sure Richie couldn't see. "My husband called you? Why would Tuck call you?"

"He needed my help to take care of a problem."

"Oh right." She laughed. "What problem could you possibly help him with?"

That stung. "You," he told her. "You're the problem."

"Me?" She walked her bike inside the garage and leaned it against the wall next to the Porsche convertible. *Whatever did that mean?*

He nodded. "Yep. Let's go inside and I'll tell you all about it."

This definitely hadn't been her plan for the evening, but she was too curious to turn him away. "Okay."

He walked past her towards the door in the garage. He reeked of smoke.

She waved a hand in front of her face. "Have you been chain smoking all afternoon?"

"Yep. Right out there on your front stoop." He smiled. "Your neighbor doesn't like me much. But I told him I was here to do some renovating, then he left me alone."

"You met Frank?"

"Well, we weren't exactly formerly introduced, but if you mean the pompous ass who lives next door, yes." He shook his head. "What happened to you? How can you live this sham?"

She opened the door to the house and entered the kitchen. "This is no sham, Richie. It's all very real." She grinned. "And very expensive. And all mine."

He scanned the room. "Nice digs," he said, not bothering to cover the jealously in his voice. He dropped onto a stool at the center island. "Get me a beer?"

"That depends. What's this all about?"

He patted the seat next to him. "Maybe you should sit down."

She didn't have time for this. She moved away from him to the other side of the counter. "Oh stop with the dramatics. Just spill."

"Just spill, she says." He laughed. "Okay, I'll spill." He leaned across the granite and looked at her eye to eye. "Tuck hired me to kill you."

She let out a snort. "You've got to be kidding me. Tuck would never do that." she narrowed her eyes at him. "What are you after this time, Richie?"

He got up, went to the refrigerator and took out a beer. "Money. Just like you," he said. "That's why you married him after all, isn't it?"

"You want money from me? For what?"

He twisted off the cap and took a swig. "So I won't kill you." He shrugged. "I wouldn't mind killing you, but what I really want is money. So, I'll make you a deal. You give me two hundred fifty grand and I won't kill you."

"You're full of shit. I don't believe you."

"Fine." Richie pulled out a mini voice recorder no bigger than a cigarette lighter and laid it on the counter. "You want proof? I'll prove it." He pressed play.

Nikki heard Tucker's voice. "I don't care how you do it, just kill her."

Then Richie's voice. "You really want me to kill your wife?"

Then Tucker's voice, "Yes, and I'll pay you."

Richie stopped the recording. "Satisfied?"

If she hadn't heard it with her own ears, she wouldn't have believed it. She knew Tucker was a selfish egomaniac, but she never thought he'd go this far. "You're playing me," she said. "You could never kill me."

"You really want to take that chance?"

"You're such a bullshitter."

He took another swig of beer. "Want to live the rest of your life looking over your shoulder?"

"I wouldn't have to. I could smell you coming."

"Suit yourself. I'll give you 'til Friday."

"Why Friday?"

"'Cause that's the day you're supposed to die."

"It's scheduled?"

"Yep. Tucker has some big meeting that will give him an alibi."

She clasped her hands together and started to pace. "I don't know. That's a lot of money to get in a week."

He let out a gaff. "Look at this place. You probably have half that in your nightstand drawer." He took another large gulp and wiped his mouth with his sleeve. "Tuck hasn't had any trouble getting it."

Her mind raced. Tucker may have arranged for an alibi, but he couldn't possibly have considered this turn of events, and she would do her best to capitalize on it. "Okay, okay. I'll have the money for you by then." Her head was spinning. She'd have to figure out a way to best them both. "Meet me Friday at 4:00 a.m. by the corner of the woods on the northwest side of Birchwood Park."

"If you're not there, I'll track you down."

"Once I give you the money, how do I know you won't come back for more?"

"Good question." He smiled and bowed. "I give you my word."

She scowled at him. "We both know what that's worth."

In that moment, her plans for that weekend had changed dramatically. She paced back and forth across the kitchen floor, considering her options. She knew she had the element of surprise on her side and decided she would take full advantage of it. That night's bike trip to Birchwood Park had taken on a whole new dimension.

CHAPTER 27

Peg assembled the group which included Isaac, Tom, and Tucker's lawyer, Perry Gronholz. Petruco preferred to stay out of the fray and took a place behind the one-way mirror.

An armed guard escorted Tucker in and placed him in the chair next to Perry Gronholz. He looked frazzled.

"Mr. Rennicke, I understand you'd like to say something regarding the murder of Richard Quiddler," Isaac began.

"That's correct," Tucker responded.

Perry stood. "Gentlemen," he interjected. "Before we begin, I'd like to speak to my client." It was quite obvious Tucker had not discussed this confession with his attorney.

"No, Perry," Tucker said to him. "I need to come clean."

Come clean? Perry thought with alarm. "Tucker, we need to talk," he said more insistently this time, leaving off the words, "before you do something stupid," but everyone knew they were implied.

Tucker pushed his horn-rimmed glasses up his nose with his middle finger. "Perry, sit down and stay out of this."

"You're making a big mistake, Tucker. As your counsel, I insist we discuss this before going any further."

"No, Perry."

He leaned down face to face with Tucker. "Your father will not be happy if you don't talk through me."

Tucker shook his head. "Not this time, Perry." They'd run his life long enough. He was going to take charge now. "I'm going to talk for myself and you should just shut up. If you don't like it, you can leave."

"Counselor," Isaac interjected. "Your client knows his rights and is ready with his confession. Shall we let him proceed?"

Perry threw up his hands and sat back down. "Fine."

"Please proceed," Isaac said to Tucker, as curious as everyone else in the room what he would be confessing to.

"I know who killed Richie," Tucker announced.

"Oh?" Isaac asked. *Interesting.* It appeared this wasn't going to be a confession after all, but an accusation. "And who is that?"

Tucker wrung his hands for all to see. "I wanted to protect her," he said. "But I just can't take the fall for this." He looked from face to face with sad eyes.

"Continue."

"My wife, Nikki. She killed Richie."

Perry sat straighter in his chair.

"And you know this because . . ." Isaac said to encourage him along.

"Richie threatened to tell the press about things she did in the past. Things they did when they were kids. Illegal things."

"Like the things you were doing in these pictures?" Isaac set the photos on the table.

It was evident Tucker took offense to that.

"No, not like that. Everybody does those things. This was something worse."

"Something worse? What?"

Tucker shifted in his seat. "I don't know what," he said. "Neither of them would tell me. But it must have been pretty bad." He looked down at his hands in his lap. "So anyway, I contacted Richie and gave him some money to keep his mouth shut."

"You gave him money to keep his mouth shut about something, but didn't know what it was?"

Tucker glared at Isaac. "Yes. I was protecting my wife," he said loudly. "Just let me talk, okay?"

Tucker obviously didn't like to be questioned. Did he expect they'd just accept his story on face value? "Okay," Isaac agreed, knowing his turn would come.

Tucker pushed the glasses back up his nose and continued with his rehearsed speech. "But Richie kept coming back for more money. Nikki found out about it and became incensed. She flew off the handle. She went berserk. I couldn't control her."

Perry nodded as Tucker described Nikki's behavior. He liked this angle.

Tucker noticed Perry's support. "Nikki could be quite uncontrollable, right Perry?"

"Most assuredly."

"Did she tell you she killed him?" Isaac asked Tucker.

"No, but she was steaming mad. And since the police discovered our gun, our hunting gear and our car were involved in the crime, I put two and two together. I understand, Detective, why you initially suspected me, but we both live in that house."

Perry sat forward in his seat and folded his hands on the table. "Given my client's revelations, I expect you will hold off on filing any charges against him."

Tucker couldn't help but smile. After all, he essentially told the truth. He didn't murder anyone, he just hired a murderer. With Perry's help, he could be off the hook, look somewhat like a hero trying to help his wife avoid embarrassment, and be rid of Nikki all in one fell swoop.

Isaac noticed Tucker's inapt smirk. *Could this be for real?* Nikki certainly had access to the gun, the clothing and the car. It also explained how Mrs. Kilbernie thought Richie returned home early that morning. Both Nikki and Richie attended the same high school. Could Nikki have been the one in the high school hoodie with the bald eagle mascot? Did she really do something so horrifying that the threat of it being revealed would be enough of a motive for murder?

"We will certainly look into Mr. Rennicke's accusations, Counselor, prior to filing any charges," Isaac said.

"Expediently, please."

"Of course." But if this was all true, then Nikki purposely set up her husband to take the fall by putting the damning photos of him in the car. Why? *Something was still missing.*

♦♦♦

Isaac and Tom left the station and crossed over to the parking lot. The sun beat down on them from straight overhead. Isaac loosened his tie.

"I have no words," Tom said. "Two very weird confessions, one right after the next. Is this typical in Minnesota, Jefe?"

"Happens all the time," Isaac said as he opened the car door.

Tom got in the passenger seat. "I'm not sure we can even call them confessions, since both confessors essentially blamed somebody else for causing the death."

"And I think both of them had a lot more to do with it than they revealed."

"Agreed."

"On that note, we need to get back to the park and take another look at the place the gun was found," Isaac said. Since he first saw the pictures, something about the scene had vexed him, and he now knew what that was.

Tom's cell phone pinged. "Ugh. It's my cooking instructor."

"Let me guess," Isaac said. "She needs your help opening a jar."

Tom laughed. "Very funny, Jefe. No, she wants me to come over and try her new lamb recipe."

"And?"

"I don't like lamb."

Once they reached the park, Tom led Isaac through the woods to the spot the gun was found. A nearby lilac bush was in full bloom and filled the air with its perfume. A pair of hummingbirds buzzed around it sucking the sweetness from the flowers.

Joyce from the forensics team arrived momentarily.

Isaac waved her over to them. "Thanks for coming on such short notice, Joyce."

"Absolutely no problem, Isaac," she said to him while smiling at Tom.

"Let's lift this top rock off and see if there are prints on the underside," Isaac said.

Joyce removed the rock with gloved hands, turned it over and dusted it for prints. It didn't take long. "Look, boys."

Sure enough, four clear prints, pointer to pinkie, showed up on either side, confirming Isaac's suspicion the rock had been placed over the top like a roof over the gun. Now Joyce could take the prints back to the lab and see if they matched any of the prints from the Rennicke's home.

As they turned to leave, a hummingbird paused over the crevice as something colorful caught its attention. Tom saw it too. "Jefe," he said. "I think I found something."

Isaac looked down to where Tom was pointing. He reached in and picked up a piece of a bright pink fingernail. He held it up in his gloved hand. It looked familiar. "Good work, Detective Bryant. I think we can be close to 99 percent certain who those prints belong to."

Isaac's cell phone pinged. It was a message from Peg. Isaac called her back.

"Isaac, they found the missing truck in an impound lot on Dupont."

"Thanks Peg. We're on our way."

They said good-bye to Joyce, and in less than fifteen minutes they were standing outside of Glen's truck. Isaac recognized it as the same truck from the gas station video. They peered in the window. A heart shaped box of chocolates sat on the front seat and a Post-it note was stuck to the center of the steering wheel. It said "Nikki — 4:00 a.m."

"Let's get this open," Isaac said.

CHAPTER 28

Inevitably, there had been a few unforeseeable glitches in her plan. Most importantly, she didn't get the money. She hadn't been able to locate Richie's car that day. It wasn't at Birchwood Park and it wasn't at his apartment. Nikki took the key she had pulled from Richie's jacket with her when she went on her rides all last week hoping she would see it along the route, but no such luck. The money wasn't in Richie's apartment either. She didn't believe he would put blood money in a bank account. *What had he done with it?* As far as she knew, Richie had not taken a trip back home to Plummer's Point, but she was considering making the trip herself to check the treehouse. That was where he always used to stash his booty. Two hundred fifty grand would be very helpful just about now.

Second, she should have given Tucker more credit. He figured it out much more quickly than she expected. He always seemed like such a puppet — unable to think for himself. But given his life was on the line, that probably changed things. It certainly had for her. She thought she'd have more time. More time to make a plausible exit from the situation.

And finally, she should have prepared an escape plan that considered the possibility she didn't find the money. What was she to do without the money?

It felt more urgent than ever to find Richie's car, so she decided to take another ride around the park, then up and down all the side streets around Richie's place — heck, she'd ride throughout the whole of Minneapolis if she had to.

She packed a bag with essentials just in case. Just in case what, she wasn't sure. But it felt like the smart thing to do.

She put on her helmet and opened the garage. As the door slowly opened, she saw two sets of shoes on the other side. Her flight instinct triggered in and she hightailed it back into the house, then immediately regretted doing so. She knew they must have seen her. Fleeing only made her look guilty.

From the driveway, Isaac and Tom watched her slip through the door. Isaac shook his head. "Let's go," he said to Tom.

They walked through the garage to the entry. Isaac knocked on the door. "Mrs. Rennicke?"

Nikki stood with her ear to the door. Her heart was pounding. *Why were they here? What had Tucker told them?* There was no use pretending she wasn't there. Whatever they wanted, she could handle it. She took a deep breath and opened the door. "Yes?"

"Nikki Rennicke," Isaac said. "You are under arrest for the murder of Richard Quiddler."

♦♦♦

Nikki's attorney laid out the case for her. He told her about Tucker's accusation, the fingerprints on the underside of the rock, the note they found in Glen's car and the love letter on the box of chocolates. Nikki surmised the money had been in the car too. It never occurred to her to take a look at the key to confirm the make of the car. Richie had owned that same old beater for the last fifteen years. It was bound to break down. She kicked herself for not taking that into consideration. Nikki folded her hands and looked down in her lap. The whole time she had been searching for the wrong car. *Damn Richie*, she thought to herself. *What was he thinking?* After all these years did he really believe she would love him back? She twirled the wedding ring around her finger. How was she going to get out of this? There had to be a way. Because one thing was certain, she'd never share the events of that morning with anyone.

♦♦♦

She stood at the edge of the tree line at 4:00 a.m. A flash of lightning lit the sky. She counted, one one thousand, two one thousand, three one thousand, four one thousand, five one-thousand. The thunder clap filled her ears. The storm was far out, but getting closer. She'd need to get going quickly to avoid the rain. *Where was he?* She pulled the hood of the hunting jacket tighter. A light flickered on the path.

She blinked her cell phone flashlight twice. "Over here," she called. "You're late."

He strode toward her. "And you're a nag."

"Come on." She ducked into the woods. "It's over there."

He ducked in behind her. "What are you doing in camo?"

"Are you kidding me? I can't afford to be seen. People might recognize me." She looked him up and down. "Why aren't you in camo? Did you even think this through?"

He shook his head. "Still the same, Nikki. This is *your* stupid plan. I didn't want to get up before dawn and tromp through the woods." He shoved his hands in his pockets.

"All this cloak and dagger nonsense. Geez, you'd think your life was on the line."

Her mouth dropped open.

"Oh, right, I guess it is." He had always needled her like this, but perhaps this time, it wasn't the best way to get what he really wanted. Yes, he wanted the money, but his heart's true desire was Nikki. During his dealings with Tucker, he realized this was his opportunity to finally win her and come away with a good chunk of cash. Once she realized she couldn't go back to Tucker, Richie could be her savior, and with the addition of this two hundred fifty grand, they'd have half a million to start their life together. Not the riches Tucker had, but then Tucker wanted her dead. "But it doesn't have to be," Richie added.

She needed to move this along. "Let's just please get this over with."

He nodded, feeling her distress. "Okay. You got the money?"

"Yes."

"Good." He looked down at the ground and kicked a rock with his shoe. "Now how about a change of plans?" He gazed up into her face. "Come with me, Nikki. We can go away together."

She threw up her arms. "Are you kidding me? You were going to kill me."

"No, you're wrong there. I was *saving* you. If I had said I wouldn't do it, Tuck would have found some other gun for hire."

The lighting flashed. One one thousand, two one thousand, three one thousand four one thousand. She shook her head and looked to the sky. "You're talking crazy."

The thunder boomed.

"I'm telling you," Richie continued. "You need to get far away from him. If you don't turn up dead today, who knows what Tucker is capable of."

She didn't have time for this. "It's going to rain soon. We need to get out of here."

Richie took her by the shoulders. "I— I love you, Nikki. I always have. You know that."

Shit. She should have seen this coming. Why didn't she see this coming? "Just stop," she said and pulled away. "You're confusing me."

"Tuck never needs to know. We'll take his money and disappear."

Nikki looked into his face and realized he wasn't going to let this go. Not until she consented.

Another flash lit the sky.

So be it. One one thousand, she counted. "Okay. I'll go with you."

His heart leapt. Finally, the revenge he'd been waiting for all his life. He'd have Tucker's money *and* Nikki — both of which should have been his all along. They all thought he didn't know, but he did. He knew who his real father was. He also knew his real father hadn't cared if he lived or died. Richie found the agreement his mother had hidden behind the loose board in the kitchen when he was looking for a place to stash the Pokemon cards he had stolen from the kid next door. He was only eleven, but he knew what it meant. That discovery also explained why his relationship with Glen was so strained. Glen treated him like a pariah. He never looked him in the eye. He never hugged him or showed him any sort of affection. According to the public records, Richie had two fathers. But according to Richie, he had none. Yet, Tucker— spoiled, selfish, Tucker, was the pride of the Rennicke family. That injustice had been eating away at Richie for fourteen years. And now he was finally able to do something about it.

"Get the bag," Nikki instructed. Two one thousand, she counted.

Richie knelt down next to the duffle.

Three one thousand. Nikki moved in behind him.

Richie's face beamed with satisfaction. *Take that, brother.*

Four one thousand. She pulled out the gun.

Good choice," Richie said. "'Cause Tuck will kill you." He reached for the handles.

The thunder clapped and she pulled the trigger. Richie's body collapsed over the bag.

"No, he won't," Nikki said with certainty. "He'll be sitting in a jail cell." She pulled the wallet and keys from Richie's pockets and yanked the duffle bag out from under him. She had to get a move on if she were going to beat the weather.

She stripped off the hunting gear and shoved it in the bag, placing it on top of the newspaper she had set there to make it appear money was piled inside. She made her way deeper into the woods and found the spot she'd prepared earlier for the gun. She placed it in the crevice making sure it wasn't visible to a passerby. It was a good twenty-five yards from the scene of the crime and hidden under a rock, so it would take some time to find. She would need the weekend up north to get the damning photographs from her dad's house, and didn't want the police to find the gun and arrest Tucker before she'd had a chance to plant the photos in his car. She removed the bloody plastic gloves. These she would discard at a gas station on the way north just in case her fingerprints could be extracted from the inside.

She found her way, as expeditiously as possible, out of the woods to the edge of the parking lot. She stopped dead in her tracks. Richie's car was not there. She started to panic. *Where was Richie's car?* She threw the duffle in the trunk of the Mercedes then ran along the parkway.

She saw no sign of his car. "Shit," she said under her breath. *Where could it be?* Hopefully the money was at his apartment, but going there would take additional time, and she had precious little.

Another flash of lighting lit the sky. One one thousand, two one thousand — she counted as she ran back to the car—three one thousand. The thunder boomed as the engine turned over. To avoid drawing attention, she followed the speed limit all the way to the Golden Dragon. Last week she had been there to pick up lunch and overheard the owner on a phone call with his security company. He complained about his broken camera and how people kept throwing their garbage in his receptacle. The biggest problem with her plan was how to rid herself of the bloody clothes once the deed was done, and this was just the solution she needed.

She jumped out, opened the lid and threw the duffle into the trash bin.

Again following the speed limit, she made her way down side streets to Richie's. She pulled up the hood on the Eagle's sweatshirt, walked swiftly down the hallway, put the key in the lock and entered the apartment.

What a dump, she thought disparagingly. There wasn't much there, so it didn't take long to search, but she left empty-handed. *Where was the money?*

The rain started as she left the parking lot.

She returned home and entered their garage at 5:35 a.m. She pulled up to the plastic bin she had placed in front of the car before she left to ensure the car was exactly as Tucker had left it the night before. She crept into the bedroom and found Tucker still out cold. The sleeping pills she had added to his martini had done the job well. She took some towels to the garage and wiped the car dry. She only hoped Tucker wouldn't notice the wet tire tracks.

She removed the scullcap covering her hair and the high school hoodie she had worn to Richie's, then went to wake Tucker.

♦♦♦

No, no one ever needed to know the details of that morning. She looked up at her attorney. "It's simple. I feared for my life. My husband had hired a hitman to kill me. It was self-defense."

CHAPTER 29

Isaac, Tom, Tucker and Perry all sat at the same table in the same places as they had the previous afternoon.

"Mr. Rennicke, Mr. Gronholz, I asked to meet with you so that I could let you know that Mrs. Rennicke has been arrested for the murder of Richard Quiddler," Isaac began.

Tucker held up his hand and Perry gave him a high five.

Tucker couldn't help but grin. This was it. He was free, rid of Nikki, and the trail of his own guilt had died along with Richie. If she accused him of hiring Richie to kill her, it would be his story against hers, and no one would believe a murderer. He would prevail. Surely he would need to do a lot of damage control, but now he had a scapegoat to take all the blame.

"Thank you, Detective," Perry said. "We had every confidence the legal process would work as it should and that Mr. Rennicke would be found innocent of the charge."

"As I have claimed since the beginning," Tucker added smugly.

"We would appreciate it if you would gather his things and release him to me immediately."

Isaac held up his hand. "First I need to also tell you that the district attorney has now filed all the charges in the case." He paused and looked back and forth between the men. "Mrs. Rennicke will be charged with first degree murder."

Tucker smiled wider.

Perry let out a sigh of relief.

"And," Isaac continued. "Mr. Rennicke is charged with conspiracy to commit murder."

Tucker pushed his glasses up his nose with his middle finger. "What?" *Shit.*

Perry sat back in his chair looking shell-shocked. *Where did this come from? Did they think Tucker was a partner in this crime?* He looked over at his client. *What had the witless little brat done now?*

"Whatever she told you, she's lying," Tucker said. *How could they charge him? They had no proof.* It was her word against his. Yet the Detective seemed so confident…. He shifted in his seat.

"Detective Scott," Perry said. "Please expound on this charge."

"Mr. Rennicke is charged with hiring Richard Quiddler, as a contract killer, to kill his wife."

"Did she tell you that?" Tucker exclaimed. "It's a lie!"

What Tucker didn't know was that, inside Glen Quiddler's truck, along with the box of chocolates and love note to Nikki, they found a padded envelope addressed to the Minneapolis Police Department that contained the recording Richie made when Tucker hired him and a letter explaining the entire plan including the dates and times of their meetings and payment information. The letter was in the form of an affidavit with a jurat. It would be admissible in court.

"Actually," Isaac said. "Richie Quiddler told us that himself."

Perry stared at his client, mouth agape, trying to figure out the best way to excuse himself from this crucifixion. The damage to Congressman Rennicke's career would be significant if not complete. It was time to hitch himself to another candidate — and time was of the essence.

"Perry, aren't you going to do anything?" Tucker whined.

♦♦♦

It had been an eventful day, and Isaac was more than happy to arrive home to find the family relaxing in the family room. He could smell Edna's apple pork chops cooking in the oven and his stomach growled in anticipation. "Edna, it smells heavenly in here," he called from the kitchen.

"Made 'em just for you, Detective."

He walked over to the railing that separated the rooms. "What would we do without you?" This reminded him of her daughters' intentions to take her away. "Are you having a good visit with your daughters?"

"Oh yes, indeed," she said. "We went out shopping yesterday."

Were they already helping her spend the inheritance? Isaac thought to himself.

"Edna was just telling me what she bought," Claudia chimed in.

"Something special?" Isaac asked.

"I should say so," Edna exclaimed. "I got one of those carpeted cat towers for Ebony."

"Oh?" Isaac said.

"Yep. It's as tall as I am!" She stood up from the sofa and put her hand to the height of her head.

"My word!" Claudia exclaimed.

"Ebony loves it," Edna said. "I put it right in front of the window and hung a bird feeder from the tree that sits just outside. He'll sit and watch the goings on nearly all day." Her blue eyes sparkled. "You know, I think he's sweet on this one particular female cardinal because he gets so excited every time she comes by. He just chatters away to beat the band." She then did an impression of Ebony chattering which made all the kids roll with laughter. "Watching him there brings me so much joy. It's the best thing I've ever bought!"

It tickled Isaac to no end to see her so giddy.

The timer went off calling Edna into the kitchen. She pulled on the oven mitt and opened the door letting the aroma fill the room. She pushed the pork chops around with a fork, covered the pan with foil, shut the oven door and reset the timer. "Another fifteen minutes should do."

"I'll get the table set," Claudia said.

Isaac pulled out a chair and gratefully sat at the kitchen table. It had been a long day. "So will the girls be staying long?"

Edna shook her head. "No, I think they'll be leaving in a couple of days." She set the oven mitt on the counter.

"Well, it was nice of them to visit," Claudia said.

"It was," Edna said, then crossed her arms over her chest. "But do you know they told me I'm too old for work?"

"They did?" Isaac and Claudia said simultaneously.

"Sure enough." She shook her head. "I don't know why they're so eager to put this old mare out to pasture."

"No," Claudia said.

Edna pulled open the refrigerator and took out the milk. "They said, 'But Mama, you don't need the money.'"

"Really," Isaac said.

Edna put her hands on her hips. "Don't they know me better 'n that? Money's not why I help out here." She held out her hands to them. "You need me, and I like feeling needed. It's as simple as that." Then she leaned over the counter and whispered, "Besides, with all that Avery is going through at her young age, I'd never leave. There are some things a child just can't share with her parents and my ears are wide open."

Isaac and Claudia shared a look. *Avery was sharing with Edna?*

"Dad!" Jacob called from the family room. "Come quick! You're on TV!"

The three of them rushed into the family room and stood in front of the TV. Sure enough, the news showed Isaac and Tom ushering Nikki to the police car.

"Another arrest rocks the Rennicke family today as the wife of Tucker Rennicke is arrested for the murder of Richard Quiddler," the newscaster said.

"It hasn't been a good week for the Rennicke family," the other anchor added.

"On a happier note," the first newscaster said. "Take a look at Crystal's Palace." An architect's rendition of a large structure with lots of glass and towering columns filled the screen. "An anonymous donor has begun plans for this new project that will provide a place for families to stay together while a family member undergoes cancer treatment. Crystal's Palace's amenities will include a fitness center, indoor swimming pool, indoor and outdoor children's park facilities, a greenhouse garden and a petting room that will include a variety of dogs, cats and bunnies. Construction is set to begin this summer."

Isaac and Claudia shared another look. "Crystal's Palace?" they asked in unison.

"Edna, have you heard of this?" Isaac asked.

"Oh yes. I already signed up to volunteer."

"Edna, dear, are you the anonymous donor?" Claudia asked.

Her blue eyes sparkled. She put her finger to her lips. "But don't go telling anybody. That will be our little secret."

"You're funding this with your inheritance?" Isaac asked.

"Inheritance?" she repeated it like it was a foreign word. "Don't be silly, I wouldn't call it an inheritance. I would never keep that for myself. It's not my money, it's Crystal's. The way I see it, she just put me in charge of it is all." She raised her eyebrows. "You know, money can do bad things to individuals, but great things for a community. And now Crystal's legacy will live on forever, bless her soul."

ABOUT THE AUTHOR

Jennifer Anderson is a paralegal with a law firm in Minneapolis. She enjoys spending her free time with her husband at their island cabin in northern Minnesota.

CPSIA information can be obtained
at www.ICGtesting.com
Printed in the USA
BVHW042139250621
610555BV00014B/284

Offensive in the Balkans

The Potential for a Wider War as a Result of Foreign Intervention in Bosnia-Herzegovina

By Yossef Bodansky

Offensive in the Balkans

is published by

International Media Corporation Ltd.
Empire House, 175 Piccadilly, Suite 1A, London W1V 9DB,
United Kingdom,

for and on behalf of

The International Strategic Studies Association
A non-profit, tax-exempt educational foundation.
PO Box 20407, Alexandria, Virginia 22320,
United States of America.

Copyright © November 1995: The International Strategic Studies Association.
All rights reserved. No part of this book may be reproduced,
stored in a retrieval system, or transmitted, in any form
or by any means, electronic, mechanical, photocopying,
recording or otherwise, without the prior
written permission of the publishers.

*The opinions expressed in this book are solely those of the author
and do not necessarily reflect the views of the members of
the Congressional Task Force on Terrorism and
Unconventional Warfare, US Congress,
or any other branch of the US
Government.*

ISBN: 0-9520070-4-5

*Additional copies of this book may be obtained from
International Media Corporation Limited,
at the above address, or by
Telephone +44(0)171-491-2044, or Facsimile +44(0)171-409-1923.*

Price:
US$15.95
UK£11.95